Ordinary Eyes

© Pamela Thornton 2018

ISBN: 978-1-7325196-0-2

Cover photo by track5 @ www.track5.co.uk

Domestic violence has no color, nor does it distinguish race or genders.

Dedicated to Wilma Martin and RaNeisha Kennedy, for knowing your worth through adversity.

Introduction

In 1969, Mercedes Hall had been released from prison where she spent 20 years for a crime of hate against her. Abuse had never been a part of her life, until the night she was dragged out of her bed and thrown on the back of a truck and driven off into the night. She had lost valuable time from raising her children and losing them and her husband to another woman taking her place.

When she stepped out of the prison walls, she was sure of what she was going to do with the rest of her life. She had encountered so many women with different reasons for spending most, or all of their time behind prison walls with no justice for their cause. Mercedes decided to be their voice.

She had known all too well the pain of injustice, and her stay in prison had shown her that injustice did not care what color you were or which class in society you were from. It only cared about the weak positions to violate.

However, Mercedes was about to take the world by the horns and change the scope of the land, making sure that life for women would never be the same again. She would risk it all, including her life, in order to bring about a change for abused women. Women from all walks of life would find their way to Mercedes who would soon become their heroine of grace.

Chapter 1

Who's Looking?

Fire blazed outside the window as loud pounding could be heard at the front door. Heavy footsteps trotted around the small neat home, with doors locked tight while the occupants quietly, but full of fear, grabbed all the children and put them into one room. Three black children and one white child, were herded into a back room, while Mercedes and her husband clinched each other's hands, not knowing why the white sheets were at their home. No --- couldn't think of one thing that could have brought them their way. But they were there, and they brought their southern way of order to their front door. There were things going on around Mercedes that no one prepared her for. Secrets of another life were being revealed to her that night. She had heard of horrific things happening to other people around her, but never thought those things would come knocking at her door.

Mercedes' husband gathered his nerves to take a peak outside, and then, he saw it. The white sheets were outside setting the last of the third crosses on fire. He also looked and saw the sheriff, someone he thought of as a friend from childhood, and an ally in adulthood. It made him feel settled for a minute as he grabbed his nerves and opened the door. Mercedes stood close behind him as she clinched his shirt tight, so tight that she didn't realize she was pulling the threads apart.

As the fire glared off her husband's body and into his eyes, he could see the Sheriff making his way towards them. He slowly stepped on the front porch and shouted, "What's this all about!" But before the Sheriff could not give an answer, he fell unconsciously from a hard sharp blow to the head --- the white sheets had rushed in on him. In the midst of the commotion, Mercedes never realized she was still holding on to his shirt as it tore, leaving a piece still in her hands.

Mercedes stood there for a moment. She could see the sheets coming from all directions, but everything was in slow motion as the men rushed in and overcame her. She was too numb to scream or cry out. And even though she could hear, she did not hear. It was if she was a deaf and mute woman, not just in her physical capacity, but also in her knowing.

Mercedes was being hauled off with no reason or understanding of what had stirred up this group of hateful men. As she passed the final person, she could see the sheriff standing with his hands on his head, looking worried, but unable to control the angry mob from throwing her on the back of the truck. She dared not to move for fear of being punched or kicked. Silence had fallen, and the only thing she could hear was the roaring of the truck's engine. She did not want to look up, but she did, to see gray, hazel, and blue eyes looking back at her.

Mercedes rode in the back of the truck quietly, until she was jolted by the quick stopping of the vehicle.

"HOLD", one of the white sheets shouted. All of the men stood up to see what was going on. It was the sheriff. He was parked in the middle of the road with a blockage of officers. Mercedes perked her ears up so she could hear more of what was going on. She could hear the clicking of rifles and hand guns as each party cocked them ready for a battle. No one wanted to shoot the other. It was more of a battle of wits, mind over matter, control of the strengths.

The sheriff stepped forward and said, "I need you all to hand over Mrs. Hall."

But the leader of the mob refused to give in to the sheriff's demands. He shouted back,

"You know we can't do that. That will be breaking the code sheriff!"

When the leader of the mob said that, immediately, the sheriff's men raised their guns and readied their aim.

"My men are prepared to shoot as soon as I let my arm down, and my arm is getting pretty tired right about now. You can either give us Mrs. Hall, or we are prepared to come over there and get her. Either way, blood will be shed tonight."

Mercedes' eyes were bucked at the words she was hearing. Surprisingly, she didn't know why she had been taken from her home so late at night. She just couldn't think of one good or bad reason. Maybe she had been mistaken for some other poor soul and was there to take their place in life's fate.

The white sheets were silent for a moment. Then, the silence was broken by the words of one of them.

"I'm not fixin' to get killed over no nigga woman. We s'pose to be doing the killing tonight." After his rambunctious rants, the man jumped off the back of the truck and started walking the opposite way. Soon, more men followed suit until there were only two left, the driver and the mob leader. They were still driven by their determination. But the sheriff shouted out again, "Well, what's it gonna be?"

The mob leader shouted back, "You know the law sheriff. And I ain't scared to fight for what I believe in."

"But are you willing to die for it", asked the Sheriff as he continued. "I know who you are, and your posse. The white sheets can't cover that up."

No one moved again, until finally Mercedes felt hands jerking her off the floor board of the truck. She was lifted up like a sack of potatoes and tossed on the ground as such.

She hit the ground so hard that her face pounded forward and she could taste blood from the hard impact. The truck that held her hostage, held her hostage no more. With her eyes looking up, Mercedes tried to get a glimpse of the scene around her, but to her disappointment, dirt was thrown into her eyes as the truck spun off in the opposite direction as the men before.

Mercedes lay there --- looking for the next set of feet or the next set of hands, wondering who was next to toss her around, who was next to spit on her or call her a black nigger. She didn't think to question the motive to her set of unsightly events anymore. Her mind was too busy processing … children, husband, jail, or worst … lynching.

The rushing of more feet could be heard as Mercedes tried to open one of her eyes. She squinted the left eye, but to no avail. Then the right. The more she tried, the muddier, grimy dirt covered the pupil of her eyes.

Finally, the feet stopped right in front of her and she could feel strong stern hands lift her off the ground and balance her to her feet. She tilted and toddled a bit before she caught her balance with one man on her right and another on her left. With the aid of the men, she hobbled on in the direction she was led until she finally reached a place and was seated gently instead of being thrown around.

Mercedes sat there in the back of a patrol car for a minute, just long enough to focus and take a few deep breaths. She still wasn't able to see clearly because of all the dirt still in her eyes. She vaguely made out the figures of men as one of them picked her legs up and placed her in the car. She wasn't bound or restrained. Mercedes just sat there, breathing and thinking.

Through all of the madness, Mercedes never forgot about her husband and children. She thought about how Ms. Janice and Mr. Bobby would have a fit if they found out the white sheets came and raided her home with lil' Katheryn Grace inside. Mercedes thought surely they would get some type of answers and justice for this night. It was their white baby they put in harm's way, so someone was going to pay the price for that.

The car soon drove off. No one said a word. The only noise being made was the thoughts that rushed through Mercedes' head. Voices that tried to rationalize her situation, voices that brought visions of fear from the people of hate, voices that brought anger to vindicate on her behalf, but the one voice she didn't hear at that time, was the voice of her LORD.

Somehow, news had gotten back that Mercedes had spanked Kathryn Grace. She would later find out where the gossip had come from. It had come from a visiting grandmother and that's how Mercedes had ended up in a crowded courtroom of her peers.

Waves of voices filled the musky smelling courtroom as Mercedes sat by a man she had never known. His pale white face did not give her any hope or any explanation of why she sat in a courtroom bound to be sentenced for God knows what. The scene around her had already predicted her future. An all-white jury sat on her right side, where some chattered with each other and others just stared proudly. Behind her were rows of more white folks who still chattered amongst each other. Even though the voices filled the room, Mercedes never interpreted one word. The voices were all meshed together. She wanted to hear something from someone. Maybe a word or two about why she sat in a courtroom ready to go down or even disappear from the only society she had ever known. Mercedes turned her head slightly, looking up into the balcony to see if she could search the black section for any familiar faces. Even though she knew they may not have been able to help her, just the sight of her husband and the kids would have given her some kind of solace.

Just then, she heard a familiar little voice, "Mommy, I wanna sit by my Nana. She's in a good seat. I can't see back here". It was Katherine Grace. Mercedes was so delighted and relieved to hear her little voice, considering that Katherine Grace was at her home when the overnight raid took place. She wanted to turn around so bad, but the intimidation in the room prevented her from getting a glimpse Katherine Grace.

Mercedes was delighted to hear the child's voice, but she would have been more delighted if she could just get a glimpse of her family. At that moment, she didn't know if they were safe or dead. The only thing she could do was hope and pray they weren't dead.

Soon voices were raised as community leaders walked in. Then, Mercedes looked over at the jury box one more time. This time she noticed some of the same men that took her from her home were seated there. She knew things were not going to be good for her. Her favor in the courtroom had flown out the door.

Finally, the court leaders were in and Mercedes' fate was about to be judged. The bailiff gave out a loud echo, "All rise for the honorable Judge Clancy!" Clancy came out with a look of seriousness, not once looking up. He looked over some papers and then asked what the charges were. A tall thin man stood up. He started stating the charges. "Excessive force, excessive force while hitting a white child, verbal abuse of a white child." He went on and on while Mercedes sat there pondering in her heart of why she was being accused of such fabricated, over-the-top charges.

Soon again, there was another twist in Mercedes demise. She was called to the stand to be questioned about the allegations that were being brought against her. The strange thing about the whole scenario was, her representative never spoke up on her behalf. She was asked about Katherine Grace and her relationship to her. Mercedes answered with short quick answers, as not to be tripped up by the questions being asked her. She tried to keep her answers to "yes" and "no" answers. The man asked her did she ever strike Katherine Grace, as to spank her. Did she ever speak loudly to her, as to scold her? Mercedes answered yes to his questions. He returned answering "Why?"

Mercedes went on to explain that Katherine Grace was in her care and whatever discipline she did for her children, she did for her as well. Mercedes said that Katherine Grace was a part of her family and she didn't feel the need to treat her any different.

At those words, the voices in the courtroom began to roar. Mercedes saw angry red faces sneer, curse, and shout at her. She became startled, not knowing what was going to happen next. The people made her seem to appear as if she was monster. Mercedes loved Katherine Grace, and had never done anything to abuse her or cross her trust, nor her parents' trust. Mercedes had always let her parents know when she spanked her or scolded her. She felt as though they were a parenting team, a force to keep order in their children's lives. It was a common thing for children to get spanked and scolded. It didn't seem strange to her. Most of the black caregivers always spanked their little white children, unless otherwise notified by their parents. At that time, Mercedes didn't know where all of this was coming from.

For a moment, there seemed to be no order in the courtroom. But after a while, the judge finally banged his gavel and shouted,

"Order!!! Everyone be quiet!"

Mercedes used to count her blessings every day, but this day, she thought she had counted her last one. The loud roar soon started to calm down and all eyes began to be focused on Mercedes again. At one point, it seemed as if she was so tuned in to the people, that she could hear what each person was thinking. All of her fears and doubts confronted her, leaving her in a state of hopelessness. From this point on, Mercedes knew she was not getting out, no matter how they represented her. She knew that "white" was gonna win and there was no justice but their own.

Mercedes' trial ended with loud voices shouting racial slurs and low hitting words of degradation. Her verdict was a twenty year sentence in prison. Only Katherine Grace and her parents stood in silence with silent tears falling down their faces, helpless to a hopeless situation.

Chapter 2

_____

A Lost Soul

Mercedes stayed at the county jail for about a week, until she was shipped off to prison without no one knowing where she was being taken but the authorities. She was allowed to see her family for the most part, but she never thought the last day would be the last day for 20 years.

On a Thursday morning in 1949, Mercedes was led out of her jail cell and onto a bus bound for her uncertain prison term. She would miss her family very much, but she did anticipate seeing them on visiting days. She knew their visits would be the only thing to keep her sane while serving time in a prison.

As she took her first step onto that horrible smelling bus, Mercedes was about to crack open. She wanted to kick, scream, and holler. She wanted to run away or even take her chances at a good wrestle with the guard. She took a pause before stepping on the bus. Then, she took a deep breath and stepped on the bus. As she got to the top of the steps, she could see that no one was on the bus but her and a white woman guard as passengers. She was looking at her with a blank face as she directed Mercedes to sit down.

"Don't think about giving me no trouble. Got a long ride ahead of us", the guard said as she pointed for Mercedes to sit down.

Mercedes sat down and moved over to the window. She thought, "I ain't gone give no one no trouble. I gotta get back to my babies and my man." She looked out the window and as the bus cranked, she put her hand on it thinking and wondering, "Where to now?"

For about an hour, Mercedes' view was nothing but fields and black bodies working them. Then, she noticed they were leaving out of the county. She had never been that far before and she didn't know if her husband had been that far either. She began to panic a little, taking deep breaths all the while thinking about where she was being taken. She didn't know what to think until she felt a strong gripping hand on her shoulder. Mercedes looked at the hand on her shoulder, then she turned around and looked in the guard's face. "Don't you die on me gal." The guard looked into Mercedes' eyes real intently, and she looked back into her eyes as to look pass her milky white face and saw her soul. Mercedes' breathing started to calm down, but she was still afraid to ask or speak a word about where she was being taken.

About four hours had passed, and Mercedes had dozed off to sleep a few times in between. The last thing her eyes had seen was trees and fields. Now, she was seeing a big opening that looked like plantation land. She could see the big trees and plenty of sugar cane as far as the eyes could see. She could see women in different areas of the place and guard houses at the fence rows, strategically placed in the sugarcane fields.

"Wake up gal. We done made it to your new home", the guard said with a loud pounding voice.

Mercedes heard the guard but never sat up nor did she make any movements to show that she was alive. Her eyes were open, but her total being was paralyzed with disappointment, fear, and pain.

When the bus stopped, the guard grabbed Mercedes by the arm and yanked her to her feet. Even though she sat at the front of the bus, Mercedes took short slow steps making it seem longer and longer for her to get off the bus. She took one step at a time knowing that's how she was gonna have to serve her 20 year sentence.

Finally, she stepped off the bus. She could see the other women prisoners. They stopped what they were doing and all eyes were focused on her. As she was being led pass them, no one said a word. They all just stared at her bowed down head. When she made it to the entrance of her building, she saw some numbers and big red letters that read, "CASA 15". At the time she did not know what it meant, but soon she would get to know the place and the people she would see every day. She also looked and saw a very large house. It was beautiful on the outside with a brick walk way that was led by trees that formed a cool breeze way. The wind from the river waters blew across her face and she could smell the muskiness of the southern air.

The guard continued to escort Mercedes through the building, until finally she stopped, pointed and said, "Here you go gal. This will be your room for the rest of your stay. Make yourself at home nah."

Mercedes looked around at the small room. The floor was made of dirt and she could see straight through the walls outside. There was a small cot sitting over in the corner with a pillow and a folded blanket sitting on top of it.

When the guard left, Mercedes sat down easy on the bed. She was all alone. She laid on her side in a fetal position and sobbed uncontrollably. She couldn't help it. No matter how much she did not to cry, she kept on crying.

Finally, Mercedes tears stopped. She had cried until she couldn't cry anymore. Her spirit was broken and she was afraid because she didn't know what to expect from this point on. As she sat there and continued to look at her new horrible place of living, she saw some eyes peeping through the holes in the wall. It was one of the other lady prisoners.

"Honey sweet peaches, are you alright?" The woman was looking as if she was scared, constantly looking around as she whispered through the holes to Mercedes.

"Yes, I'm alright", Mercedes replied as she stooped down to whisper back to the woman.

The woman gently slid a heart-shaped rope through one of the holes, then quickly ran off. Mercedes held it in her hands. As she examined it, she saw that it was made out of the husk of sugar cane. Mercedes took her hand and ran the shape between her fingers. The only thing she could think of was her children and her husband.

"How could this have happened to me", she thought. A few more tears began to fall, but she quickly wiped them away. She sat on the bed for a while longer, not knowing that time was passing faster and faster.

All of sudden, she heard a man's voice holler out and screams from a woman's voice. Mercedes looked out the window. She saw a big black man whipping the woman that had given her the heat-shaped sugar cane husk. He whipped her violently, then he started hitting her with his fist. He beat her so, until she could not scream anymore. The other women just stood around with faces of sorrow. Soon, he shouted out "What y'all looking at? Get back to work before I tear into another one of y'all worthless trifling wenches."

The women quickly scattered, leaving the beaten woman on the ground, alone and maimed. The man turned around and looked towards Mercedes way. She quickly ducked from the window, hoping he did not see her. Her heart was beating so fast that she thought she was gonna have to go catch it.

Mercedes peeped through one of the holes in the wall. She could see that the big man was gone and some of the women were picking the woman up. They carried her into the building where she was staying. Mercedes could see the women as they passed by her door and brought the lady to the room next to her. Some of the women were sobbing as they laid the woman down. Mercedes stood in the doorway as other women got rags and water to clean the woman's wounded face and body.

Just then, an older black woman walked in. She was limping a little, but she made her way through the women and to the wounded woman.

She said, "Lawd, Shuggie. What he done to you this time?"

The older woman gathered some of the water and poured it across the woman's face. She patted it dry, reached into her pocket and pulled out some kind of salve. She began to rub it across each of the woman's wounds. Mercedes stood in the distance as she watched the woman's hands gently work on the woman. She had old wrinkled hands with scars that told her story. The old woman was gentle with the woman as she hummed a tune to her all the while rubbing her with the utmost care and compassion. As the old woman continued, the woman opened her eyes, then her mouth, and said softly, "Sweet Helena."

All of a sudden, the old woman stopped what she was doing and answered her back. "What you saying Shuggie?" There was no response. Everyone stood there, waiting. Seconds felt like hours, but there was not another response. Tears began to run down the old woman's face and soon tears ran down everyone's face. It was a bitter mourning for the woman as death had given her peace and eternal rest.

Mercedes went back to her room with a sorrowful heart and a fearful heart as well. She had seen a woman die right before her eyes and didn't know what was waiting on her outside of those doors. She sat there on her bed until she started seeing the women come out of the room one by one. The old woman never came out. She stayed there and mourned over the woman's body. Mercedes could hear her praying and every now and then, she would hear her sing a hymn. The sounds that came from that room gave Mercedes a little comfort that God was true. There was not much sleep for Mercedes as she lay on her cot listening to the old woman's memorial service all night.

When morning came, the sunlight kissed Mercedes' smooth dark skin. Its rays were warm against her face, but suddenly she was awakened by the shuffling coming from the other room. Mercedes made her way to the entrance of her room door to see the big black man and some other officers carrying the stiff body of the woman out the door. As they passed by, Mercedes caught herself as she was looking in the man's eyes. Fear gripped her soul while she slowly backed up out of their way. She quickly went to the holes in the wall in order to look outside, for she wanted to know where they were going to take the body. Mercedes took her time, looking through the biggest hole she could find. She saw all the women standing around, some crying and others quietly consoling each other. The men took the body of the dead woman and threw it on the back of a tuck, took a white sheet and wrapped her body up tightly.

When the truck was out of sight, Mercedes looked off to the east. She saw the rest of the women heading to the sugarcane fields in order to get their work day started. One of the women beckoned for her to come. Since it was her first day, Mercedes did not know what to expect on a plantation. She started out with a slow walk, but soon got in a haste after seeing the big black man who had beaten the woman to death.

After making it to the women, one of the women said, "Welcome to Hell. Alright now, it's time to get you started to know how to get this suga cane cut. Cause you gotta cut it right or you won't get no sleep tonight. We gone show you how to do it for a few days, then, you on yo' own."

Mercedes didn't quite know what she meant when she said she might not get any sleep at night, but she was quiet sure it had something to do with the big black man. It looked like he was running the place, and used fear to control the women.

The woman introduced herself as Addie, Addie from upstate. Then she went on to introduce some of the other women.

"This here is Barbara, Delsi, Carolyn, May Helen, and Rocky. She 'bout the only one 'ole Big Blackie Boone won't mess with. Only cause she like the same thing he like."

All the women gave out a gust of a laugh as Rockie replied, "Sure do. And I have had a little of all y'all too."

When Rockie said that, Mercedes put her head down in shame, because she had never heard women talk the way these women talked. Right then and there, she knew she was out of her element. She had stepped into a whole new world, a world that was totally different from where she was from.

After the introductions, the hilarious laughs and strange conversations, the women began to show Mercedes how things went around the plantation. They took her down each row and showed her the right way to cut the sugar cane and the wrong way to cut it. They made it look easy, but when Mercedes picked up that long blade, it nearly made her lose her balance. She swung the blade the best she knew how, but the sugar cane was still standing and had not been moved. "Well --- we got some work to do", said Addie with a sharp grin. All the other women began to chuckle and snigger.

"You got to aim at it, size it up", said Addie. Addie put the blade close to the bottom, careful not to miss. She reared back a little, then swung precisely. It was a perfect cut.

"Now, if you get this right, you want have to worry about 'ole Big Blackie Boone messing with ya too much."

Before long, three days had passed and Mercedes still hadn't got the hang of throwing her blade at the bottom of the sugar cane. Her body was sore and her emotions were bottled up, ready to explode at any time. During those days, she would see Blackie Boone walking in the distance looking at the previous spots where she had hacked into the sugar cane. She would see him pull one of the women to the side and scold them harshly. They never put the blame on her. They only continued to help her find the right fit of the blade and the right position for her to cut. But Mercedes knew it was a matter of time before she would find herself before ole Blackie Boone.

Around the fifth day of working with the sugar cane, Mercedes could feel her muscles begin to relax a little and the soreness was easing up some. She began to feel good about her progress, but still held her family in heart. Everything was still fresh. The memories of her tumultuous events played in her mind, in her sleep, and every time she was alone. Most of the time, she would cry herself to sleep.

As she stood there in deep thought, suddenly, Mercedes was caught by surprise as she was being dragged off into the sugarcane. Her heart beat fast, as it seemed her breath was taken away. She dropped her blade, and as she was being dragged away, she could see one of her shoes come off. She could not scream because her mouth was covered tightly.

When her movement stopped, she hit the ground with a "thump". Shaken up, Mercedes didn't move. She knew well who it was. She knew it was Blackie Boone. Mercedes just sat there. She didn't know what he was getting ready to do, so she braced herself for whatever was getting ready to take place.

"Get up", shouted his deep raggedy voice. Mercedes slowly moved one foot under her and then the other foot without the shoe. She stood and faced him. Blackie Boone walked towards her and then around her, looking with inspection. He stood behind Mercedes, then grabbed her vigorously and pulled her close.

"Yeeeesss. I got plans for you", he said, breathing hard into her ear. "These old biddies trying to protect you, but I see you. I see you hacking up my good sugar cane. That, you gone have to pay for."

Mercedes could feel him rising behind her, making her feel eerie and violated.

He ran his hands through her hair, purposefully getting his fingers tangled in her curls.

Then, he grabbed a fist full and yanked her head closer to his mouth saying, "You belong to this plantation now, and mostly, you belong to me. I know everything there is to know around here and everything to know about you. You gone be my little night cap. Since those whores schooling you on everything, make sure they school you on that."

When Blackie Boone had finished molesting her and threatening her, he forcefully threw Mercedes on the ground and left. She sat there looking at him vanish in the sugar cane with the intentions of crying, and she did. She cried for herself, for her family, and for the poor state of the women on that plantation. But then, Mercedes got up mad.

Her day had started off good for the most part, but ended not so well. By the time the sun had set, Mercedes was shaken up, angry, and kind of scared. She didn't stop to talk to the women. Instead, she went to her room to freshen up for the night.

After she had finished, Addie stopped by Mercedes' door and asked if she was going to join them for supper. Mercedes agreed, but she did not join in the conversation much. She listened to the women as they told their stories of how they came to be on the prison plantation.

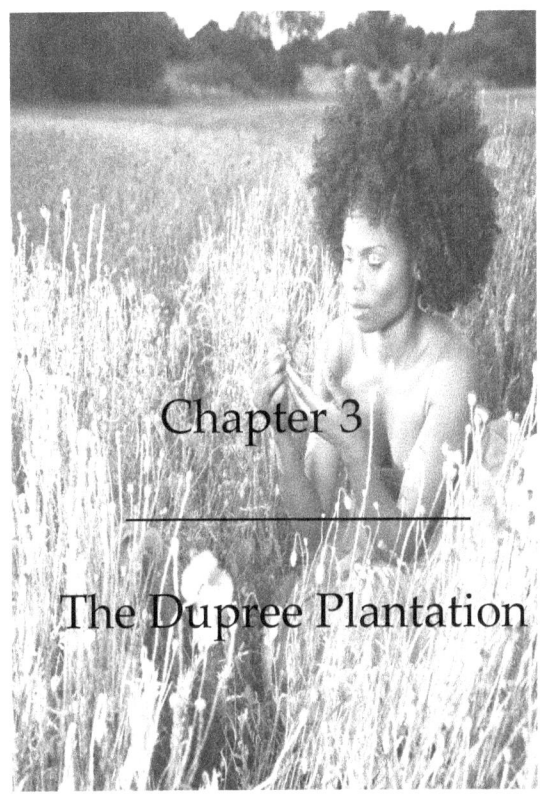

Chapter 3

The Dupree Plantation

The Dupree plantation was named after the Dupre family of France. As time passed, it finally came to an end with Josephine Dupree, who made it into one of the largest sugar cane plantations in the south. Josephine was one of the richest plantation owners who operated the sugar business with a stern hand and had a strong league of plantation managers. Three hundred acres of sugar cane, two hundred acres for living and almost a hundred slave workers (some rented and some indentured). She planted her fortune by the mighty Mississippi River alongside some of the other wealthy plantation owners.

Josephine had married young into the Lefleur family, but sadly her husband of only two years, mysteriously died leaving Josephine with the tedious task of running such a large sugar business. However, it was not an unfamiliar task for her, only because she had been raised from generations of plantation and business owning family. During her youth, Josephine would travel back and forth to France where her family had a large estate there as well. She got a chance to experience the good and bad sides of the sugar business from her grandparents and parents --- slaves being bought and sold, and working in harsh conditions. They were even beaten or worse, killed.

As a young woman running a large sugar plantation, Josephine encountered many men competitors along the way. There were not too many times that went by that she would not encounter the swindles of greedy counterparts and manipulative businessmen. This made her more cunning and wise to the hearts of men. Josephine never remarried, for she always kept the thoughts of men-in-calling as ravenous wolves in sheep clothing. No man could break her, because the fear of losing was what kept her from losing.

But time would change all of that. The great war between the North and the South was moving its way towards her and all the other plantation owners. The talks of union soldiers disrupting their way of life were beginning to creep into everyone's home, including the slaves. The slaves were beginning to run away and join the fight for freedom, thus making all the plantation owners lose money and property. However, Josephine Dupree was not without a plan. She knew that if all else failed, she would move back to France and take her fortune with her.

She could see it coming. A failing economy was on its way for all plantation owners, whether rice, cotton, tobacco, or sugar cane. Either way, the Dupree Plantation was gonna lose, but the Dupree name and its fortune would live for generations to come.

When the time came, there was a great plunder to all the plantations. Those that resisted, were either killed or court marshaled. There was no peace for the plantation owners, but Josephine stayed her ground until the very end. No one was gonna take it all. Even though she had her business fixed in France, she still wanted to see her family legacy through to the end. When it was all over, Josephine took her last look at the Dupree Sugar Plantation, and walked away. No regrets and no grieving, she bid farewell and accepted the new change that had over taken the American south.

Years gave way to the plantation as desertion and emptiness allowed the beautiful house that sat in the front of empty fields to waste away. Only memories remained of a thriving sugar business of Josephine Dupree, until the state of Louisiana decided to expand on growing the prison industry, thus keeping the sugar business going for state revenue.

At first, there were many men who work the Dupree Sugar Plantation as free laborers, but soon the men were moved to a more contained prison area and the plantation became an only women's facility. There were no more than seventy five women held on the plantation and fifty bunking houses for living. Some were close by each other and others were scattered across the plantation, sectioned off in groups.

The time they spent there was not supposed to have been no more than a two to five year detention, but the people who ran the prison saw fit for the women to have longer sentences. They did this because it wasn't too often that women went to prison, so they kept them there longer for labor in the sugar fields. It was only another form of slavery. When the women would come to the plantation, they would have a due date for their release, but when that date would come, they would only end up in disappointment to find that their dates had been extended. It had become a place of hell and a point of no return. Some had spent their lives on the plantation. Some had died from work exhaustion in the hard southern heat or the cold frigid temperatures. Either way, hard labor and long hours sent the Dupree Plantation back in the times of slavery. Even though the times were changing around them, the plantation was still stuck in time.

Chapter 4

Our Souls Have Eyes

Supper time was filled with stories and memories of the women's past lives before they came to live on the Dupree plantation. Laughter filled their small living quarters as the group of women crowed the place for good food, conversation, and a little relaxation before they had to get up and work hard labor day in and day out again. It was a time to bond with each other and revive each other. Mercedes didn't know what to think as she sat close to the door watching each of the ladies' characters be displayed as uniquely as they could be.

Addie stood up and said, "Now that we have had good food, it's time to revive our souls once again."

All the women began to grab each other's hands. They even grabbed Mercedes' hand as Addie continued her speech.

"It's also a time to remember the one soul we just lost. This is your time to mourn for that soul. This is your time to mourn for your soul. This is the time to mourn for all the poor souls that have landed in this horrible place of hell. Don't leave one tear un-cried. Don't leave your soul without a mourn, because your soul needs to cry out. It needs to release the pain. It needs to release the hurt."

Delsi started out with a long moan in her cry. Then, May Helen followed. Soon, the whole room was in a state of wailing and mourning. There were heavy tears from each woman. Their wailing, mourning, and tears seemed to come from the soul. Even Rocky had a few tears to come streaming down from her stone looking face. Every soul had a story behind those tears, even Mercedes.

The mourning and the wailing session lasted for fifteen to thirty minutes, depending on how deep the pain was. Mercedes wiped her eyes as she began to hear a rhythmic clapping of hands. It was a transitioning of her soul. The sound grabbed her deep, like water being poured into a thirsty mouth.

The stopping of the hands led Addie back to another speech.

"Now that we have once again poured the soul out, it is time to put back in the soul." Addie started out with a loud belting of words.

"I am stronger today. I am more brilliant today. I am the strong tree of earth, with many branches, with long strong roots. I am the root of the earth, created in love, set in grace. I am connected to heaven and earth. I am the prize they are seeking to win. Great grander am I. Great grander am I!"

One by one, the women began to chant the poetic words that seemed to give Mercedes a little more hope. As she listened to the chant, the words rocked her soul gently. Her hand began to squeeze the next hand tightly as

Mercedes' body began to sway back and forth to the melodic sound of the women's unified voices. She began to see every good things that had happened in her life and she began to see every bad thing that happened also.

The unity of the women gave Mercedes strength on the inside, making her think of her family and giving her great hope of getting out of prison as soon as she could. Maybe the days would pass by faster. The thoughts of living free again danced through her head --- the thoughts of her family being back together again made her tingle on the inside. She knew there was light at the end of her tunnel of turmoil. There was a great sigh released from her body as she sat there and soaked in the atmosphere, an atmosphere of love and hope. She opened her eyes and gazed at each of the women, looking at them, seeing how they had left that place of prison and entered into a place of freedom. They talked free. They walked free. They even moved free. There was something on the inside of them that made the plantation seemed invisible, and Mercedes knew that if she stayed close enough, she could have the same experience.

There were no downward faces when the gathering was over. Only smiles and laughter as each woman left with their own peace to carry them on for the next day.

At sunrise, Mercedes felt refreshed, ready to go cut sugarcane. Binding her hair in four locks, she took a long white scarf and tied her head up. One leg at a time, she slid her legs in the large overall she was given upon arriving at the plantation and buttoned up her old plaid shirt, then her rubber boots to compliment her rugged attire.

When she walked out the door, she met the rest of the ladies, who was ready and refreshed. They all walked passed the big house to the back where breakfast was waiting in the kitchen. Each of them were handed a small sack, each filled with a biscuit, and a piece of fatback. No one complained, as they walked down the pathways laughing and talking, eating their morning meal. Once they reached the place where they would be cutting, their blades were already sharpened, laid out for them for their daily tasks ahead.

Mercedes stood in the field, put her hand to her brow, and thought, "Where does it end?" The sugar cane was from the east to the west, north to the south. She wondered how long it would take for them to cut all the sugar cane before they went to the processing mills. She stood there for a minute looking as far as her eyes could see, until she looked into the eyes of ole Blackie Boone. He was standing afar off with his eyes tuned into hers. Mercedes quickly looked away and rejoined the women.

"What wrong with you child? Looks like you seen a ghost", said Addie. Mercedes looked back and so did Addie. They both saw Blackie Boone still looking their way, but she grabbed Mercedes by the arm and told her, "Come on. We ain't fixing to let him ruin our day. Let's get to cutting girls. Got a long day ahead of us."

One by one, they picked up their blades and went their ways, disappearing but still being heard. They were still able to talk and laugh with each other through the purple skinned stalks as each woman slung their blades perfectly while the sugar cane fell making them visible again. This routine kept on throughout the day. By the time the noon bell had rung, Mercedes was cutting in rhythm with the team of ladies.

They all gathered back together while the lunch truck met them where they were. When they saw who was driving and passing out the lunches, their smiles turned to frowns. It was Blackie Boone again, there to intimidate

Mercedes. At first, the women didn't know that's what was going on. He passed out the lunches without cracking a smile or saying a word, and the ladies took their lunches without looking at him or smiling either. There was an open spot in the field where they went and sat. They dared not talk about Blackie Boone in his presence. They waited until he had left and the truck was out of sight before they uttered one word about him.

"I'm glad he has taken his big ole black rhinoceros looking self on. I wonder why he passing out our lunch. Wonder where the regular guy is", inquired May Helen.

"I don't know", said Delsi, "but I sure hope this ain't gone be a regular thing. He gives me the creeps every time he comes around."

Rockie put her food down and looked at Mercedes. "I know why he passing out our food", she replied. "There's fresh meat on the plantation."

All the women stopped eating. Addie just stared at the ground as the other women began to look worried also. Addie looked at Mercedes. She got up and went to her.

"There's no way we gone lose another one to that wild monster of a man. He has no soul and if he ever start forcing you, he's gonna eventually kill you. Sweet Helena lost her poor precious Shuggie to the hands of him."

Then Addie turned around, looked at the women and said, "We gotta protect this one. Enough is enough. I've been on this plantation for ten years and I've seen so many beaten to death and so many disappearing. This has got to stop."

All the women agreed and vowed to do their best to protect Mercedes from the hands of Blackie Boone. While they finished their lunches, the women came up with a plan to protect the then young Mercedes.

When it was night time and all the women had finished their laundry, supper, and baths, they turned in for the night, but not without executing their plan. The women had decided to take turns sleeping in Mercedes' room while she stayed in another cabin for safety and rest. Each night the women waited for Blackie Boone to come to them, but he never appeared.

Two months had passed, and the women began to feel a little relaxed, seeing that Blackie Boone had not visited Mercedes' cabin within that time. So they decided to let her go back to staying in her own cabin. Mercedes was thankful for all the help the women had shown her and she was thankful to God that she didn't have to endure any harm at the hands of Blackie Boone. They thought that maybe he had lost interest, or maybe he had found another woman to terrorize on the other side of the plantation. No one knew, and no one really cared, as long as he stayed away from their part of the plantation.

When the women were nearing the end of cutting all the sugar cane, winter was blowing in the north winds deep down to the south. The plantation and its workers were getting ready to shift to the mills. There, the women would be processing sugar and syrup. The buses would be loaded down, going in the mornings and coming back in the evenings. Mercedes didn't know what to expect, so she would stayed on the women's heels for lessons of the trade.

On the last day of harvesting the sugarcane, the women were glad that they would be going to the mills. It was a chance for them to get out of the cold and for some of them to see men. Even though the women worked hard, they also got a chance to mix and mingle with men from other plantations who were free, but had no choice but to stay on the plantation and work old debts off. Sometimes, the mixing and mingling would lead to marriage and help the women find a place to stay when they would hopefully be released from their plantation prison sentence.

The day had ended just like days before. But the nights were longer and the days had become shorter. Mercedes was kind of happy because she knew they would have a week off before starting hard work again. She walked away from the fields with happy thoughts, thoughts of finding comfort in a place that kept her separated from her family, a place where distance was far away, but her mind kept her close to home.

However, when Mercedes walked through her doors, she saw a big black figure standing in her doorway. It was Blackie Boone.

He stood there with a smirk grin as Mercedes stopped in her tracks at the sight of him.

"You might as well come on in nah. I been waiting on you for my night cap", he insisted.

Mercedes wanted to run, but where would she run too. She thought about the women, knowing that no one expected him to be back on the prowl for her. While she stood there, Blackie Boone kept talking, delivering his fearful words towards her. Mercedes was afraid, but his words seemed to have power over her as her feet gradually walked towards him. By the time she reach him, he violently grabbed her and punched her in the face. She hit the floor really hard. She tried to pick up her dizzy head. But Blackie Boone kicked her head back to the floor.

This time she stayed down, going in and out of consciousness. He put his foot on her head, all the while unloosening his pants.

While Mercedes was in and out of consciousness, she could see him as he picked her up, threw her on the bed, and beat her totally unconscious. Mercedes did not feel the punishing pain Blackie Boone had put on her body. He unleashed his sexual rage on her that night, making it hard for anyone to recognize her. No more did she have that young beauty she came to the plantation with, nor did she have that beautiful smile to match it.

No one had seen nor heard from Mercedes the next morning. The women knew it was not like her to be late coming out the cabin. Nevertheless, Addie took it upon herself to go over and see what the matter was. When she walked through the door, she saw a lifeless creature, lying on the floor with a swollen head and dried blood all over. With tears in her eyes, Addie knelt down to check Mercedes for life. She was still amongst the land of the living, but barely. Mercedes had a broken nose and two black eyes to match her busted lips. Addie wept with great vigor, and knew all too well who was behind this dilemma. She knew something was going to have to be done.

When the other women heard the news, they wept with vigor as well, but immediately began to nurse Mercedes' wounds. They each felt so many emotions. Pain and anger flooded their souls as they all sat around looking at the sinful mess that was lying in front of them. Everyone knew something was going to have to be done, but no one knew what. Rockie was filed with anger. She walked through the plantation looking for Blackie Boone. She didn't know what she was going do or say, but she was willing to take a chance to confront him. But no one saw him for the rest of the week as Addie and her friends took turns helping to get Mercedes well.

Gradually, over time, Mercedes' features began to come back as the swelling went down.

Sweet Helena was informed about the tragedy and offered her benevolent services. She cooked soups and made natural teas for healing. Even though she had just lost her only child Shuggie, and the pain was all too familiar, she put her tears aside to help save someone else.

As she gently fed Mercedes, she talked softly to her. "I wish my Shuggie would have had the strength and courage to leave that old Blackie Boone alone. But he wouldn't have left her alone though. He beat my child to death. When they first started their mingling, I was kinda happy, thought maybe that would have been her way outta this hell hole. But it wasn't. He made hell a little hotter for her."

Sweet Helena helped Mercedes sip some tea and continued, "I been here on this plantation for almost thirty years. I've seen a lot of things go on with these women and to these women. Sometimes it looked like a playing field for the men. There were times they would just take one of the girls right there in the sugar cane fields. Wasn't no shame in their souls. That's how I got my Shuggie. Right there in the sugarcane fields."

Mercedes quietly listened as Sweet Helena's aged voice continued to tell her stories of her days on the Dupre Sugar Plantation. Mercedes didn't want to become a victim of that life for 20 years. She knew she still had to have her sanity because she longed for the day to leave the sugar plantation and be united with her family again.

Sweet Helena kept talking about the life and times on the plantation. Then, she turned in a serious way and said, "You know, I don't think some people will ever change until they take their last breath. They'll be that way for all their lives."

Shaking her head, she turned around and continued to help nurse Mercedes back to health, not knowing she had planted a seed in some of the women's head.

There was a lengthy time before Mercedes could get back on her feet, and before she could say she was in perfect health. Her face healed very well, leaving almost no signs of abuse on her body. Since the big Blackie Boone ordeal, most everyone knew Mercedes was to be singled out by him. No one wanted to lose another woman off the plantation, so the women put their heads together for some justice of their own. Plan by plan, and plot by plot, the women wanted Blackie Boone gone and they had figured out how. They thought that maybe peace would befall the plantation, but it didn't.

The day Mercedes was to go back to working in the mills, winter had brought a cold that the Deep South had never felt before. She had to bundle up but did not have enough clothes to do so. She thought it would have been a good idea to go borrow some from the other women. As she walked the pathway to Addie's cabin, she grabbed the little clothing she had on tightly, trying to keep every bit of warmth she could inside. The sun was slowly rising as she walked up the steps and began to knock. She stood there and waited on Addie to open the door. There was no answer, but the door opened to invite her in.

Mercedes gave a little shout, then a big shout, "Addie it's me. Came to borrow clothes if you have any." There still was no answer. Mercedes pushed the door opened as she continue to make herself known while she entered the neat little cabin. She continued to call out, but there was still no answer. Since Addie was not in her cabin, Mercedes tried the other women's cabins as well, and found that their cabins were empty too.

By the time Mercedes had finished looking for the women, the sun had risen in its early morning fullness. She could not understand where they had gone so early. She knew that the work van had not left because their work materials were still sitting by the doors.

So, Mercedes began her walk back to her cabin. As she walked, she could see something hanging in the big tree in the middle of the plantation. She could see people beginning to gather around. Mercedes walked a little closer as the cold wind blew which added more chills to her body. But the cold winter wind had nothing on the chills she got when she finally arrived to the tree. She fell to her knees as she looked at three bodies hanging, limp, crooked, and stiff. It was Addie, Rockie, and Delsi. Their bodies swung on the long mossy trees as the winter wind gave them a sway back and forth. Their souls never traveled off the plantation again. When time stopped for them, their souls were trapped, stopped by death, never to see anything else. What was the last thing their souls saw? Who could have brought such tragedy to their lives?

Chapter 5

Addie

My Soul Has Eyes

My daddy taught me how to hunt. Didn't know where that man came from, but he was my daddy. In my mind, there wasn't nothing he couldn't do. He taught me how to raise a gun and shoot it. He also taught me how to throw a knife and hit my target head on, and with that same knife, he taught me how to skin and gut my kill, clean it and cook it too. Yelp, that was my daddy.

I didn't know anything bad about my daddy, but underneath, he was hustler, hustling with the wrong kind of people. He had his hands in a lot things, things I was too young to understand or just too naïve to the fact that my daddy was my hero. He could not do any wrong in my eyes. He brought home many wonderful things for me and my mother. I don't think there wasn't anything we didn't have that the white folks didn't. We lived in the colored part of town, but we lived a wealthy life. Daddy made sure of that. I can still remember him, tall, brown skin, slender build. He kept a part in his hair. He said it made him look fine, and that was alright with me. Whenever daddy was home, he kept laughter in the house with his old corny jokes while at the same time, swooning my mother.

As I grew up, my father began to get down on his luck with money. Whatever he had done to get it, his way of getting it wasn't working any more. Strange people began to stop by the house looking for him. They even left threats to harm our family if he didn't pay.

By the time I had turned sixteen, my daddy was dead. Yes, someone had come to collect their debt and his life was the payment. As usual, we never got any justice for his life. Never knew who killed him, nor did we ever hear a rumor about it. He was just dead! That's it --- dead! The only thing I had was memories, things my soul kept recorded, things that brought me a little happiness whenever things seemed to get hard around the way.

Me and my mother maintained for the most part. Daddy had hidden money back off in the woods and any time things got tight round the house, mama would leave late at night and get a little bit. She wouldn't get a lot. Just enough to maintain. That kept the questions down from the ear hustlers and gossipers.

I don't think anybody loved my daddy the way I loved him. Might be foolish talk, but it's real to me. That's why I am on this plantation. I killed a man for talking against my daddy. He gone tell me that that wasn't my real daddy --- that he was. I wasn't trying to hear no one tell me that Matthew "Slim" Connor wasn't my daddy. I can't remember nothing nor no one else ever being around me and my mother, but my daddy. So, I asked him was he trying to say that my mother was whore. Sounds like to me that's what was coming out of his mouth. Whether he meant that or not, that's what it sounded like to me. I didn't know what angle he was playing at, but I had mine set on my pistol tucked away nicely in my bosom. Everyone says he was drunk, doing that drunk talk, but I wasn't. I didn't care. I pulled out my pistol and shot him dead right there on Annie Mae's juke joint floor. I wasn't about to give up my memories of my daddy for some old drunk fool's illusions. So here I am and here I be, right here on Dupree Sugar Plantation.

Chapter 6

Rockie

My Soul Has Eyes

I don't know why it was so hot the day I decided to help my brother rob the downtown drug store. This year made three years I been down here cutting and throwing sugar cane day in and day out. Before I came here, I was living, living a life of fun with my brother.

Mama said when she had one baby, she didn't know another one was gone come out of there squealing and crying. She said I shocked her and the doctors. She said she asked them, "Now what I'm gone do with two little babies at the same time?"

Well, I don't know what she thought she was gone do at that time, but she managed to raise me and my brother and she kept us fed real well. She raised me as a girl, but the more I became a woman, I didn't feel like one. I felt more like my brother. I began to dress like him and wear his clothes. I even began to date women like him. No one understood me but him. He was my best friend and he kept all my secrets from our mother, and our mother always kept her secrets from us.

One day my brother came to me with some heart breaking news. He said he had over-heard our mother talking with the landlord. They were discussing the matter of the rent. Who knew she was three months behind? She kept things hidden from us very well. She had until the end of the month before we would be out on the streets. The days went by so fast. It seemed like the end of the month was tomorrow.

During the course of that time, I began to think about the things that were going on around us. I saw the injustices, the biases from my own people, and the way BLACK was ostracized in our society. Jobs were hard to come by, so there was no law to protect BLACK, no union to protect BLACK jobs, only twisted laws to keep us down, laws and people put in place for colored people to beg and struggle. I saw my uncles put in jail, all because they looked at a white man in the eyes, or for just walking on the wrong side of the road. I've even witnessed people being picked up for nothing and never seen again.

After thinking and communicating our thoughts, finally my brother came up with a plan and I was down for whatever plan he had. However, I didn't know it was a plan to rob a store. I thought we would go sell something or do some odd jobs around town, but the plan was to rob the general store. But it was worth it for our mother's sake.

The night before was kind of strange. There was no pat-rollers on the roads and the general store had closed early. The job seemed easy for us, or so we thought. We made it to the back of the store, where my brother picked the lock while I was the look out. Soon I heard the clicking sound of the lock releasing and then we were in. It was dark inside. Only the moonlight lit our way to where the money was. As we eased our slender bodies around each corner, careful not to knock anything over, we finally made it to the stored cash in the back office. It was if it was inviting us to take it. There was no lock and key protecting it. It was just laying out in plain sight. As soon as my brother picked the money up, he stood up, looked at me and smiled. I smiled back. We were happy to have it and soon wanted to be on our way. The same way we eased through the store, was the same way we eased back to the back door. But as soon as we opened the door, bright lights blinded us and the county was there pointing guns at us. We were surprised and overwhelmed!

I don't know which way they took my brother, but I ended up here. And I don't know what has become of our mother. Don't know if she even knows where I'm at or what jail he's in or if he's still alive. So, for the price of our mother, I have to do these hard twenty. God only knows what my brother is going through. But the Dupree Plantation has my name now.

Chapter 7

Delsi

My Soul Have Eyes

People have always told me that I had my mother's eyes. I never believed them because I had never seen my mother's eyes. I only seen my father's eyes. No one ever told me that she was a colored woman. The only colored woman I ever loved was our maid, Mamie. She took care of me all the days of my life before I ended up here.

Every family has secrets they don't ever want anyone to know about. My family was like that. I lived in a white house with a white family and a black maid that told me "I had my mother's eyes" almost every day. She said it with a smile and sometimes with tears in her eyes.

At first, I never asked questions, but as I grew older, I wanted to know my mother. I never saw any pictures around the house, nor did I ever hear my father talk about her in any detail. He would only say, "You're beautiful, just like your mother."

In my teenage years, sometimes I would look for my mother in the mirrors, searching my face over, looking for any signs that might give me a clue of what she looked like.

One day Mamie caught me staring intently in the mirror. She called out to me while laying neatly folded clothes on the bed, "What you trying to find in that mirror?" I told her I was trying to find any signs of my mother. Just a glimpse or even a hint of her. Mildly and yet confident in her answer, Mamie slowly walked over to me and gently knelt down beside me.

She put her face next to mine while staring in the mirror with me and said, "You don't have to try and find your mother. Every time you look in the mirror, you're looking at her."

By the time I turned seventeen, Mamie was getting ready to make her transition to heaven. She began to get a little slow and then sick. She was not able to do the things she used to, so I pitched in to help around the house. The things I didn't know, Mamie coached me on them, especially the cooking. She gave me all her kitchen secrets, and then her other secrets. Some secrets are meant to be just that, secrets. But I guess death makes a person tell it all since they don't have to live with carrying the secret no more.

Mamie called me close. She could hardly talk, better yet, catch her soft breaths. She talked with a whisper, though I was still able to understand everything she said. She started off blunt and to the point by telling me that my mother was a colored woman. She said she wasn't all colored though because she had a black mama and that she was my mother's mother. That made Mamie my grandmother. The one who took care of me all my life, was my grandmother.

I sat there, still and speechless, as the words of Mamie seeped out of her old wrinkled brown lips. She continued to tell me that she was a widowed woman before my mother was born. Her colored husband had been killed a year before, so that left her penniless and lonely. Mamie said she had to survive, so she started working in a night club down the old Peoria road where the mighty Mississippi brought in all kinds of people from all over the place. She worked as a waitress and also she worked for favors on the side. Her favors got her to be a favorite with one white army sergeant who was stationed not far from the Memphis line.

The young sergeant would make frequent visit to see Mamie, at first bringing her more money than what she was asking for. Sometimes she didn't have to do anything for his financial exchanges. He would just tell her to open her hands, place the money in it, and gently close her hands. No one knew that their non-conjugal visits had started to turn into a romantic love affair. This went on for about a month, and then, it was no more.

The sergeant left the area, going on about his military commitments. There was no way that they could have had a future anyway. Besides, he was white and Mamie was colored. And even though he was gone for good, he still left a part of him with her. Mamie said every bit of his love was in her. It was my mother growing on the inside. She said with her being pregnant, it helped her not to miss his sweet presence as much, because every part of that baby kept him close to her heart.

Even though Mamie was in a blissful time, she knew she would have to protect my mother's history of racial identity. No one would ever know that her baby had a white father. And they never did.

History has a way of repeating itself. A colored woman and a white man falls in love again, and I'm a part of their union. Mamie told me that my mother died giving birth to me. A bloody mess she was, while the midwives had a time trying to get a breeched baby out of her.

Mamie said she don't think anyone expected for me to look just like a white girl. As I grew, my hair never curled and my skin never tanned. It only burned in the hot sun. She said I was a little blondish red head mess walking around with a dark colored woman. She had to go to my father and find a solution because they didn't want it turning into a problem. Mamie said she couldn't bring me to town because everyone would surely start with the question and the gossiping, then the speculations that would turn into violent night raids. She said they just kept me tucked away until she and my father were able to come to some kind of resolution.

Their plan was simple. My father moved south towards the Gulf of Mississippi and brought me and Mamie along. Their plan worked out just fine --- father, daughter, and maid. No one knew that Mamie was my grandmother, including me. I didn't ask questions and no one volunteered answers. Everything was as it looked.

I had been raised as a white person. Nothing about me gave any indications that I had colored blood in my veins, but when Mamie had taken her last breaths of truth to tell me who I really was, there was no need to pretend I didn't know about society. We can know better but still do foolish things, like live a lie by marrying a white man and having a colored child. I ended up on this plantation because I lived as a white person. The law said I was guilty. So here I am on the Dupree plantation with no family, not even my colored child.

Chapter 8

Parts of the Soul

What can hurt the soul so bad than to see the people you love hanging from a tree? To see her new found friends leave the world just as quickly as she had met them, tore a hole in Mercedes' soul. It took something away from her as she realized that she was in a heartless and gutless place. She had never seen a hanging, only heard about them. She was torn and broken over the deaths of her three friends but was yet drawn to their lifeless bodies as they hung from the low lying branches of the tree. She approached the bodies, staring at the broken necks and the bulging eyes from which their souls had departed. Mercedes saw the mangled torsos and twisted mouths and legs as blood still dripped from the mouths of women who were gone to soon.

She stood there just like the others that stood there afraid to cry or attempt to cut the bodies down. But her soul was deeply grieved. Mercedes gave out a loud cry like only her soul could give. It was a deep and painful cry. She ran up to each body with great attempts to lift them up from the ropes that bound them to the tree, hoping in vain that life was still in at least one of them. With no hope of help from the others that stood around, she soon gave out of strength and collapsed to the ground, and wept for her friends.

There was the sound of footsteps approaching, and instantly Mercedes was snatch off the ground and tossed afar. It was Blackie Boone. He stood tall with a prideful look as he placed his hands on his sides and gave a short speech.

"These here gals needed to be made an example of. You all that have been here for a while knows we don't tolerate any insubordination. This here is PRISON! It ain't no convalescent home, nor is it a vacation home. These here prisoners made an attempt on my life and you know that ain't gone go unpunished down here on the plantation. I don't know why y'all standing around like you ain't seen no dead bodies hanging from this here tree. Ain't nothing new."

Blackie Boone stopped talking for a few seconds and made his way towards Mercedes to put the final touches on his speech. He stared her right in the eyes and said with a deep gut wrenching voice, "And if I find out anyone else was involved, they'll be joining their friends." Then he walked off, making sure that the dirt of his heels flew in her face.

Mercedes looked around at the people as they walked off seeming not to have a care in the world about her friends. There seemed to be no justice or any sympathizers, until she felt a gentle hand and a light old voice from behind. It was Sweet Helena.

"Get up. We gotta keep moving. Ain't no time to mourn them right now. We can do that later. Right now we gotta keep this sugar cane plantation running so we can keep our hides and our lives. Pull it together now."

Sweet Helena encouraged and motivated Mercedes to get up and go to work. There was no way she thought she could work through the day knowing what she had seen and knowing that Blackie Boone had killed her friends.

The work day went by slow and steady, all the while Mercedes played that early morning scene over and over in her mind. She wondered how people could be so cruel and live such hateful lives. It was as if they weren't human, like they had the souls of animals. She continued to work, careful not to let Blackie Boone see her sorrowful heart. Everyone kept their composure. No one else showed any signs of grief as they worked the sugar mill all day. There was no laughter, no talking, and no teasing, only work. Nevertheless, Mercedes anticipated on the end of the day so she could go to her quarters and finish grieving the rest of the night.

As the end of the work day was coming to an end, Sweet Helena eased by and told Mercedes to meet her at her quarters as soon as the night fell. So when night fell, Mercedes did just that. She used the cover of the night to cloak her way down to Sweet Helena's quarters. When she got there, she saw a large number of people there. She was met by one of the workers who cautiously guided her to where Sweet Helena was. She saw almost everyone there, but her heart was low because she didn't find Delsi, Rockie, nor Addie's face amongst the crowd. Carolyn and Barbara were there, but she found it kind of strange that she didn't see May Helen amongst the people.

Mercedes kept walking until she made her way to where Sweet Helena was. They greeted each other with a soft hug as Sweet Helena guided Mercedes to a seat by her.

There was so many voices in the room, including the ones in Mercedes's head. Sweet Helena gathered both her hands and began to pray or Mercedes. She knew that her stay on the plantation was gonna be a long hard stay, so God would have to be her strength. Sweet Helena knew that Blackie Boone would not let Mercedes be, for her own child died at his hands and so did Delsi, Rockie, and Addie. It was not going to be easy for her, nor her last time encountering death. Sweet Helena also knew that she would need God's protection for this life or the one to come because the plantation was known for taking lives and loved ones would never hear from or see their families again.

Mercedes soon found out that the gathering was a mourning meeting, a memorial gathering for the three that were murdered. No one mentioned the murderer, but everyone knew that Blackie Boone was behind the murders. He was always getting away with some kind of evil, even killing Shuggie in broad daylight. Mercedes was his target now and he was aiming at her, first trying to instill fear in her, and then controlling her with it.

Sweet Helena had seen it all too often. She had been on the plantation all her life, not by lawful incarceration but she was a resident there since childhood. Her parents were debtors, and no matter how hard they worked to pay off their debts, they got further and further behind. That was only because they couldn't read and write and the plantation knew it. That was its way of keeping free labor. But as Sweet Helena grew up, she began to realize that reading and writing was a way to stand toe to toe with the system of the plantation. She found a way to befriend a white overseer, who taught her how to read and write. Not only did he teach her how to read and write, they also had a romantic relationship that brought about a beautiful baby girl, Shuggie. Together, they worked the system and Sweet Helena secured her place on the plantation. She had seen so many things, and saw the hearts of men. They were evil and fed off the selfishness of it.

But now, it was time for a change. She was getting older and knew her days would end sooner than others. She had to find a way to school Mercedes so she could live and not die at the hands of the plantation. She knew how things had worked out for her, so she hoped that the same thing would work for Mercedes. There was no guarantee that her closeness to Mercedes was going to work, because she knew that Mercedes would still have to use her wit and wisdom for the things that were to come her way. Sweet Helena knew how Mercedes anticipated seeing her family again, but deep down she knew it was a slim chance of that happening. No one hardly ever saw their families. Some would not see them until the day of their release, and most of the times the families would have moved on because they would think their loved ones were dead.

After the memorial of the three, Sweet Helena advised Mercedes to stay a few nights with her. She knew she wasn't going to be able to stay for long periods of time because Blackie Boone would be on the prowl for her. But Sweet Helena just needed her stay just long enough to instill something in her for the twenty years ahead. The death of the three was still fresh, so Blackie Boone would not come to her right away. That would give Sweet Helena a little leeway.

For the first night, Sweet Helena took her time and told Mercedes all about her history and her time on the plantation. She told her of her love and lose, about the good times and the horrible times. There were no corners cut to what Sweet Helena would tell Mercedes, and no mercy as Mercedes cringed at the stories that fell off her lips.

"No one is safe from these mens. Some of them only take work here because the plantation is filled with womens. It's like a playground for them, but if you can find a descent one, take your chance. It may be your only way of being safe from some of the horrors of Blackie Boone."

After spending the first night with Sweet Helena, Mercedes thought and thought. Her mind was all over the place. She wanted to go home so bad, she thought about running away and wanted it to become a reality so bad. Most of her hope had left her, but a small glimpse was still there to help her hold on. She thought about her courage and how small it was. She tried to pull it together on the days she worked in the sugar mill. She tried to smile and conversate as much as she could, but every time she saw or thought about Blackie Boone, she would fall to pieces.

The second night Mercedes stayed with Sweet Helena, they used the moonlight to go pick special flowers. Some were green and others were a bleeding red in the middle.

"These are my Caladiums. I have used these many times as a defense against any unwanted hands."

Soon, they moved to another part of the plantation and Sweet Helena had Mercedes to go down a steep hill and pick her a different kind of flower. "Now, those are called 'Dumb Cane'. Ain't nothing sweet about the cane part. These will come in handy as well."

Sweet Helena went on teaching Mercedes that night about things that were twisted, yet helpful. She showed her how to grind the plants down and make powder. She also showed her how use it on unwanted men if she couldn't get it in their mouths.

"I tried to teach this to my Shuggie, but her mind was too slow for thinking." Sweet Helena kept grinding and instructing Mercedes as she talked her through the night hours. When Mercedes did lay down, her mind was all over the place again and sleep hardly came. She thought, how could she poison someone or harm someone in a way that Blackie Boone did.

But time would always tell a different story, because time was all she had. All she could do was work and pray that within her twenty year sentence, she would be able to come off the plantation alive and intact. Sweet Helena was all she had as far as hope. She still had her faith in God, but she also knew that Sweet Helena was sent to help her along the way.

After a month of waiting to see if Blackie Boone would make his move on her, Mercedes became a little relaxed. She had begun to build walls of strength from the time spent with Sweet Helena. She had all the information for keeping herself alive, well, and sane from any kind of predatory men, but was hoping she would not have to use any of it.

Mercedes sat on her bed and pulled out the heart Shuggie had given her when she first arrived on the plantation. She held it in her hands and then held it close to her heart as she thought about the family she left behind. She missed them so much. She didn't know if they were alright or if the clan had come after them also. Mercedes didn't know where to get answers from or who she could talk to about contacting them.

While she sat there staring into nowhere, she heard a light tap at her door. It was May Helen. Mercedes had not seen her since before the others were killed. She didn't know if she had went missing or was working for someone else, because the plantation would hire out women, from time to time, to other businesses. So that was a possibility but not fact.

While May Helen greeted Mercedes, she asked, "What are you up to? Haven't seen you awhile." Mercedes replied softly, "I was thinking the same thing about you. Haven't seen you since our friends was murdered." May Helen went on to say that she was afraid for her life and asked for a work hire – out. She sounded pretty convincing to Mercedes, therefore earning her trust as they continued to talk a while longer. They talked about the situation and the things that supposedly happened the night the women got caught and was hanged.

Mary Helen went on to tell a gruesome story about that night. She went on to tell her how the plan the women had was set in motion. Blackie Boone was good as buried, but couldn't understand how he got out of the dirty grave. She went on to say that by the time they had gotten back to their quarters, washed up, and in bed, someone had kicked the door in. The loud sound of the door being kicked in startled everyone in the cabins, even those who were asleep in the quarters close by heard the noise. May Helen went on to tell her side of the story. Mercedes sat there with tears in her eyes, listening to every detail.   May Helen told Mercedes a story of half-truth. She never mentioned the fact that she was working with Blackie Boone all along. She was just as evil and cunning as he was, doing anything he asked just to save her life and live comfortable while on the plantation. May Helen stayed close to Mercedes and went and reported everything she could about Mercedes and the others. She was partly responsible for the deaths of the three and the hell Mercedes had encountered and the hell she would encounter in the future.

When the conversation was over, Mercedes sat there for a few more moments thinking. She knew something had to be done about the conditions on the plantation. She wondered what to do before she had to encounter Blackie Boone again or some other man who thought they had to prove their power of authority over her. She looked around at her surroundings. She looked at the holes in her walls, the deteriorating conditions she lived in. She knew she would be there a while, so she decided to make it a little more livable and decent. There seemed to be no hope there, but a little hope was all she seemed to muster up, and that was all she needed.

When the sun rose again, Mercedes headed down to Sweet Helena's cabin before the work trucks got loaded for the day. She had her to braid her hair in three corn-rows in honor of her three friends that died trying to give justice on her behalf. She told Sweet Helena that justice had to be served on their behalf and she was going to make her life count for something.

Sweet Helena did as Mercedes requested of her, taking her time to part the hair and braid each braid neatly as possible. Her hands felt good to Mercedes as memories flooded her mind from the past. With her eyes closed, her thoughts took her away from her present state of imprisonment to freedom of the past and her hopeful future. She knew she had a long time away from her family, but her motivation to change things on the plantation would help her with getting through each day. Sweet Helena had taught her many things, but one thing she had brought with her was a praying heart. She was thankful for all she had learned from her mentor, but she knew that her state in life would require a higher power.

Chapter 9

A Change Has Come to the Dupree

Plantation

Changes had come to the plantation. Changes that would allow Mercedes to be free to express her ideas. Mercedes found herself before a board of all white men who stared meaninglessly at her. She sat in front of them quietly as she waited to see what they wanted. She had never been before this council before, so the mystery that stirred her was about to be revealed.

One of the men flipped opened a small folder. He read her criminal history, then looked up and asked her, "How long have you been on this plantation Ms. Mercedes Hall?"

Mercedes responded politely, "It's been almost 11 years sir."

"How do you feel now than when you first came here?"

Mercedes dropped her head, then looked at each man sitting in front of her. She thought carefully about what she was getting ready to say. Then, courage overpowered her fears as she began to talk.

"I take full responsibility for my past actions as I do for my actions now. I cannot say it's been an easy task living here on this plantation called hell. There was no relief of pain and torture for the women who get up day and night ---- who work in harsh conditions, whether scorching summers or harsh winters, having our dignity stripped and identity suppressed by the hands of sex thirsty men, who tend on doing whatever to us and whenever they want to has made the conditions here as tolerable than the places we have come from. So, how do I feel now from when I first came here? --- I know I have been changed. "

"The voice of justice is never silent", Mercedes continued. "It may be just a whisper, but it is always heard. Some have learned their lessons and others are learning a lesson that has taught them that their innocence hasn't been heard. I have written many letters over the years to our Governor asking for help and a start-up of counseling sessions. I have not had a response to either. These sessions would at least give the women some kind of hope while they reside here on the plantation."

The men sat there with no expressions on their faces. Mercedes didn't know if she had said the wrong things or not. All she knew was, she had spoken from her heart --- not to offend anyone, but to shine the light on the conditions there and to get a little help from the outside.

The man closed his folder and stood up, and the others followed his lead. They told her they would see her in another year, then she was escorted back to her quarters. This was the beginning of the change.

Mercedes sat down on her bed and began to think of the outcome of this first meeting. She wondered would any change come to the plantation as she looked up and saw Blackie Boone standing at her door as times before. He was her torturer. For 11 years she endured his harsh sexual acts and his furious beatings. But she had managed to keep the beast in him calm over the years. She simply did what he had asked and prayed all the while he did what he did to her.

It had been six months from the time Mercedes had met with the men, and surprisingly she received a letter form the Governor's office. It was unusual for her to get any kind of mail, so she wasted no time opening the piece of mail. She pulled the piece of paper out quickly, wasting no time unfolding it. Her eyes grasped the heading that read, "From the Desk of the Governor".

"To Mercedes Hall:

There is a reform going on in the state of Louisiana that is bringing about a change in the prison system. I have received your letters and have turned my attention to your concerns about the women on the Dupree Sugar Plantation.

I have granted your request for a program consisting of group sessions that will be beneficial for building up persons, and helping persons to cope with life and current situations. The program will be fully funded by the state of Louisiana.

By the end of the year, the old staff will be replaced and a new staff will be added. ---"

When Mercedes read that part, she dropped the paper. It seemed to put her in a daze as she thought about living without Blackie Boone. At that moment, she didn't care about being in prison. She was only thinking about how life would be without him on the plantation.

Shaking her daze off, Mercedes reached down, picked the paper up, and continued to read the somewhat wonderful news. As she continued reading to the last line, she sat down on her bed speechless, hoping and praying that a change was really about to come the Dupree Sugar Plantation.

As the days went by, new people began to show up around the plantation and they were a bit friendlier as well. The sight of the old workers began to diminish and so did Blackie Boone. It wasn't a good week after the arrival of the letter that he was not seen any more. The excitement that flooded Mercedes heart was joyful and thankfulness at the same time. After all the excitement, she was overly ready to start group sessions with the women. Not only that, she wanted to start classes for cooking, sewing, and many other things. It was things she wanted the women to know whenever they were to leave the plantation --- that way, they would be able to make a living outside of prison.

Time started telling the story and making Mercedes' prayers true. For the last six months, things were really going fast for her. During this time, she received a knock on her door. When she opened it, it was the white woman who rode with her on the bus to the plantation. Mercedes was puzzled at first, but soon found out the woman was there to take her to a better place.

"Ma'am, I need you to gather your things. You are getting ready to be moved from this place", the lady said with a sternness in her voice.

When Mercedes heard that, she was over joyed, yet confused, then sad. She then asked the woman, "Where is it that I'm going?"

"You're going north to the Louisiana Women's State Penitentiary. It's the Governor's request", the woman continued.

Mercedes thought, "The Governor's request." She was happy that she was able to get the attention of the most powerful man in the state, but then dreaded the departure. She didn't want to leave all the women she had befriended, and she definitely didn't want to leave Sweet Helena. She was the one who prayed her through all the rapes and the beatings, all the low rating and hard work. She remembered those days when she just knew she would die. But Sweet Helena told her she wasn't having that. She told Mercedes that not another woman was gonna die on her watch, especially her.

Mercedes turned to the lady and asked, "Is it possible for me to go and say a few good-byes before I leave?"

The woman looked at her sternly, but nevertheless she gave her permission to go and say good bye. "You got one hour. After that, you need to be loaded up for departure."

That one hour was fine with Mercedes, even though she would have liked a whole day. She finished packing her things, which was not much, and started her way down to Sweet Helena's cabin. Tears began to fall as she took each step. She began to count her steps in her head, thinking about how long it would take her to get to her friend.

When she finally got to the door, Sweet Helena had already known the purpose of her visit. The tears continued to fall from Mercedes' eyes, but Sweet Helena only smiled and grabbed her by the hands. She said, "Tell me about it."

Mercedes rested her head on Sweet Helena's lap and said, "God has answered my prayers, but not in the way I was expecting."

"In what way were you expecting?" Sweet Helena looked down at Mercedes and smiled as she waiting for her response.

"I was expecting for the Governor to grant my request for starting a support group for the women here on the plantation. Part of that was answered, but now I have been moved to the Louisiana State Women's Penitentiary. I wanted to stay here and make a difference."

Mercedes sobbed for a few minutes as she poured her heart out to Sweet Helena. But nothing she said moved Sweet Helena to join in with her sobbing. Yet, she picked Mercedes' head up and said, "Dear sweet soul. There is nothing to be sorrowful for. God did answer your prayers and more. Soon, all the women on this plantation will be joining you. But you will be the first to go. They going to get you ready for the journey ahead. Baby girl, God is sending you to prepare the way, just like He did John for Jesus."

Sweet Helena then raised her hand towards the ceiling and then raised her voice, "Everything is gonna be alright. He's not a failing God."

With that being said, Mercedes was kind of excited but yet wondered how Sweet Helena knew all of that.

"I been around this place a long time. I got my ways of getting everything I need to know."

Then, Mercedes inquired about ole Blackie Boone. Sweet Helena told her she wouldn't have to worry about him terrorizing another woman on that plantation or any other prison camp. "There has been a changing of the guards", she said excitedly. At those words, Mercedes joined in the excitement as well.

There was no turning back after that. Before the hour was over, Mercedes had said her warm good-bye's and was on her way. She awaited her new journey --- hopeful that she was starting anew.

When Mercedes arrived to the new facility, she was amazed at the things she saw. She saw that the women looked more refreshed and less stressed. Even though they worked daily, it was not the work that broke their backs. The women had specific jobs assigned to them weekly. Some days, some worked the fields, some days some did the grounds gardening. Mercedes even noticed that in the cold months there were green houses for growing food. She had never seen anything like it. This new place was a long way from the Dupree Sugar Plantation and the things she saw made her question the place, "Is this a prison or a retreat get-away?"

By her 12th year of being incarcerated, Mercedes had been trained in full capacity of group sessions and small business matters.

This was a big feat for her and her social status, but that was something she didn't have time to worry about. There were all kinds of women walking through those prison doors, and each one of them uniquely broken. It was her job to help them serve their time and find a little dignity of their own. She was glad that there was no one raping them and no one taking them off to never be seen again. Mercedes had found her greater place and life calling.

Even though she had been trained for her role in the prison, nothing really had prepared her for the real life experience. Soon after she had finished her time of training, Mercedes walked the halls of the prison, anxious for her first mentor or group session. The only thing about it, she had to find women who wanted to be engaged in that kind of setting.

As the days went by, they turned into weeks. She would have become discouraged, but her will was too strong to let her. She knew there were women who needed the group sessions and that led her to rethink her strategy. She had to get the word out and she knew exactly how she would do it.

Mercedes went to her advisers and trainers, letting them know that she was looking for willing women to participate in her group sessions --- and it wasn't long before she was stopped by one advisers who told her that there was a woman she had recommended to the group. Her name was Eula.

Eula was a rather large woman, and her self-esteem was very low. She did not love herself after looking at how she used to look and her looks at that moment. She didn't love herself, so she didn't have any reason to love anyone else --- nor did she think anyone had a reason to love her. There was always a bit of isolation on Eula's part.

The encounter with Eula was not the encounter Mercedes had hoped for. She had played it all in her mind. She was hoping for a loving, kind, gentle Eula. Instead, she got the opposite.

The day Eula walked in the room with Mercedes, there was no one there but the two. She stood at the door for a moment before Mercedes noticed her. When Mercedes did see Eula, she beckoned for her to come in. Eula looked in, and then left. But that still didn't discourage Mercedes, because she knew the behavior Eula was displaying. She knew she was dealing with a runner, a person who had been mistreated and abused. Mercedes knew she was dealing with an emotional malnourished woman and it would take a while to break the mold.

Everyday Mercedes went to the group session room and everyday Eula would stand at the door and then leave. So one day, Mercedes decided to try and hold a conversation with Eula. Like before, Eula came and stood at the door, waiting on Mercedes to look up. But, she never did.

Instead, Mercedes said, "You are safe in here and whatever we talk about will not leave this room." For a moment, it looked like Eula was gonna come in, but she didn't. She left just like the other times.

The next day, Eula came to the room door and to her surprise, Mercedes was not there. She didn't know what to think until she heard a voice from behind her say, "Don't worry. I'm still here for you."

Immediately, Eula stepped into the room and made her way to one of the empty chairs. Her size made it difficult for her to sit in just one chair, so Mercedes gently pulled another chair up to the other one for Eula to sit more comfortably. She didn't smile or show any kind of facial expression, nor did she allow Eula to see her face no more than seconds. But it didn't matter. The damage that was inside of Eula had already been done.

Eula shouted, "You're making fun of me, aren't you?" Eula shouted to the top of her voice again, "You think I'm a fat slob. I know you do. I know how people see me."

She spoke with anger and pain, yet Mercedes spoke with kindness and skill. While Eula continued to hurl out all kinds of profane words, Mercedes simply turned around, sat a distance and waited for Eula to calm down a bit. She sat there with no real expression --- only taking notes, looking up at Eula every now and again.

Finally, the shouting stopped. Eula was breathing hard, and while she sat there looking at Mercedes like an angry bull, Mercedes caught Eula's attention with these words, "So, what do you think of yourself? I've heard you say what others say about you, but what do you think about Eula?"

With a snappy, "I don't know", Eula folded her arms and held on to her angry face. Mercedes looked at Eula from head to toe and found something that she admired about her outward appearance.

"Well guess what", Mercedes replied with a small smile, "I don't know about you, but I see a lot about you that's beautiful. First of all, look at that hair. Sometimes I wish I had beautiful long, straight hair like that. Mine is the curly type. I don't care how many times I straighten it out, this hair insists on curling back up. And the color --- most women have to dye their hair to get that silky black look. I bet it would look wonderful in a bun or just some curls."

As Mercedes complimented Eula on her hair, Eula's frown began to disappear. Mercedes knew she had gotten to a soft spot. Eula still didn't break for a smile, but deep down was enjoying the admiration Mercedes was giving her. Her arms began to unfold, but not with a smile yet. "I got this old hair from my mama. But I got all this white skin from my pops."

"Well Eula, I think your white skin is beautiful as well. It makes your blue eyes more noticeable", Mercedes responded.

This time, Eula's answers were calmer and engaging. It didn't matter if she didn't talk much. Mercedes was just happy she got Eula to open up a little. And a little she did. There was not much conversation after that and soon Eula was on her way out the door. Mercedes was taught it would take some time to see results from some of the women, but she didn't expect to see some so soon from Eula.

The next day group sessions were closed. Mercedes took that time to sit outside and watch the women carry on their daily duties and play. As she sat there, she saw Eula in the distance. The closer she looked, the more

Mercedes could see there was something different about her. It was her hair. Eula had put her beautiful hair up in a bun and added a few curls as well. Mercedes did not approach her, yet she gave an unnoticeable smile.

When Mercedes turned in her first report on Eula, the state of Louisiana saw that the program was working for the most part. But that was only one woman. She knew she would have to continue to show results in order for the resources to continue to come into the prison. But in the meantime, she would continue to work with what she had, and that was Eula.

In the next group meeting, Eula came through the door a little more confident than she did before. She still had a shy stand-offish demeanor, but Mercedes could see the change. She made sure she made a big to-do about Eula's hair. She made everything about the meeting focus directly on Eula. Mercedes said things like, "Your hair is beautiful", and "You are really gifted with hair". Her praises made Eula open up more and more. Soon, they were talking about her family back at home --- her sisters and brother, her mother and father, even the place she was raised. Eula told Mercedes before she came to the prison she made a living as a hair dresser. Mercedes was so happy she could see the light in Eula, because in the past, the women on the Dupree plantation didn't have any hope. She wanted so badly to ask how she got to the prison, but she didn't want to push too fast so soon. Mercedes knew eventually Eula would tell her. Right now, she was content with Eula opening up and beginning a process of healing.

Chapter 10

Life Can't Wait

As days and months passed, Mercedes had not seen any of the familiar faces the Dupree Plantation, nor had she heard from her dear friend Sweet Helena. She thought about her often and missed her as well. She wondered if the Governor had changed his mind about getting the women transferred to the new facility.

Mercedes took it upon herself to go and inquire about the transfer. The people in the facility didn't hesitate to give her the information she needed. They told her that the women from the Dupree Plantation would have been there sooner, but they did not have any paperwork. The state of Louisiana had to find out who each woman was and where they were from. In the process, the state had to contact relatives to see if these people really came from those places. They could not go on word-of-mouth. The state had to have some kind of proof. There was no kind of order over there. The state of Louisiana had to launch a full investigation because some women had disappeared without any trace. Even if the women had died there, there were no graves to show that they had been there. There were also women who had been in the prison longer than they were supposed to have been. So, some of the same people that held them captive, were now going to prison themselves.

When Mercedes was hearing all of this, she wondered and then asked, "Did anyone contact my family?" The woman pulled out a folder as Mercedes sat there in a daze, thinking about her husband and children. Her thoughts were still stuck in the past, not realizing that life was not waiting on her, and it was not the same after twelve years in prison. When the woman opened Mercedes' folder, she told her that her family had been contacted and they did confirm her identity --- that was one of the reasons she departed the plantation so quickly.

Mercedes' response was, "Is the address still 84 Red River?" The woman answered yes and Mercedes was thrown into deeper thought.

"How long has that been?" Mercedes asked while starring off into the distance, waiting for a quick response. The woman answered her slowly as she noticed how Mercedes' countenance had changed from excited to somber and sad. She told her that it had been days before the departure from the plantation also.

There was no word from Mercedes' family. The last time she had seen them she was being led out of a courtroom and put in jail. At that moment, her thoughts were so distorted that she couldn't remember if her husband had said he would come visit or not. It was not that Mercedes didn't forget her family. With no word from them and no way of contacting them from the plantation, she thought they had forgotten about her.

When she made it back to her room, Mercedes sobbed uncontrollably. Her tears wet her pillow as well as her bed while she cried for her broken state of life. She had been ripped from her family, her life torn apart from the familiar.

As she laid starring at the ceiling, she decided to write a letter to her family in hopes on getting a response.   At first, she didn't know what to write, but then, her words began to flow from within --- deep from her soul. There were so many feelings flooding the letter and she let them all out, except the feeling of anger. Yes, it was there also. She felt abandoned and left, but she didn't let it out because who knew the reason for her family not trying to contacting her. The Dupree

Plantation was so marred and corrupt, no one heard from their loved ones.

When she had written the letter, she didn't send it off immediately. She took her time and read over it several times, hoping she had said everything she wanted to say. She wanted it to be perfect, just like she wanted her life back. Mercedes waited until the next day before sending her letter. She didn't mention ole Blackie Boone and the horrors he had brought to her life. She only wanted them to know that she was still in existence and she missed them very much.

After sending the letter, Mercedes didn't know what to expect. She didn't know if her family would write back or not, nor if they would visit. A sense of depression began to set in. She began to think about how unfair life could be for the colored people, then she thought about how unfair life could be for the woman. Yes, the woman. Even the colored man had begun to be abusive towards their women. There was no barrier for the woman, not a safe place to run. Even though she had not experienced some of the things she had seen and heard from other women, but she had experienced this abuse from ole Blackie Boone.

Mercedes knew she had made a vow to build women up, no matter what color they were, so being in a depressed state was not a long time option for her. The morning made a difference as she had slept her depression off. The only thing left for her to do about the matter, was to wait. And that she did.

It had been three months later when Mercedes received a letter in the mail. It was addressed to her with her husband's name on it. Excitement and fear held her as she starred at the piece of mail in her hands. She was happy to get an answer, but her feelings were telling her that she would not like what she was about to read.

She slowly opened the letter, carefully unfolding the one page paper. Her eyes scanned each line slowly, careful not to miss one word, and when she had gotten to the last word, tears began to flow. Her husband thought she was dead and had married another woman. He had also included that he was on his way to see her, alone, and he would try and explain their life's dilemma. Mercedes took the small letter and tucked it under her bed. She sat for a while in deep thought, thinking about her children wondering what they might have gone through without a mother. She thought about how they probably had to grow up fast in order to help their father around house.

Not long after receiving the letter, distant thunder had awakened Mercedes one Tuesday morning. Just like the weather was on the way, so was her long awaited visitor. She really didn't know what day her husband would be coming, so every day she looked at the post mark date and counted the days from there. She also primped herself for his arrival because she wanted their encounter to be something special if possible. She kept her corn rolls fresh and her skin shiny and black. Even though the pain of her husband getting married again was stuck in her heart, she held on to the hope that he wasn't.

Eventually, Mercedes got the notice she had been waiting for. It was him. Before walking through the door to greet him, Mercedes peeked out of the door's small glass window. She saw him sitting there, looking around. He looked just as nervous and anxious as she was.

Finally, she bravely opened the door and made her way over to where he was sitting. When he saw her, he stood and embraced her with a big hug. In his mind, it was an unbelievable sight. He had no idea that she was still around or even alive. As they both sat down, they unintentionally started their conversation together, but gave order to the conversation by letting Mercedes go first.

"I have so many questions. I don't know where to start", Mercedes said in a shy manner.

Her husband insisted, "You can start anywhere you like. You deserve to know all the answers you desire."

Mercedes' questions began to flow out one by one as her husband listened, careful to answer her politely as possible. There was no easy way for her to accept her reality. She cried and sobbed again and again as most of his answers broke her heart over and over.

This was the conclusion of that chapter in her life:

As time went on, there was no word from Mercedes. Her husband told her, at first, he had exhausted every way of finding her. The parish police gave him the run around, telling him that she was in this or that place. He said that he had heard about the Dupree plantation and tried his best to get there, but no one would give him the right to come and see her. After six years, he said that he received a letter in the mail, and when he opened it, it was a death certificate.

Her husband pulled the piece of paper out from the top of his shirt pocket, handed it to Mercedes and let her read it. It was dated 1955 and signed with Blackie Boone's name on it and the warden of Dupree plantation. When she read it, it shook Mercedes to her core, and at that moment hate entered her heart. It was not consuming hate, but just enough to spark a fire deep down in her soul and make her tears dry up.

As she sat there, her husband continued to tell her of his journey without her. He said that after that, he was raising their children alone and he knew he needed a woman to help around the house while he continued to work. He didn't want to lose their home and didn't want their children going to work for white folks in the kitchens nor in the fields. He wanted them to have a choice, and a good choice, so eventually he married again.

"The children took to her good, but nothing could have ever replaced you. They often spoke of you and missed you very much", her husband gently said as he held is head down shamefully.

Mercedes didn't care to hear that either. The more he spoke of another woman, the more hate spilled over the love she had for him. Life had handed her a bad deal, and at that moment, she had lost all control of her path of helping other women. The group sessions would turn out to be a part of her healing therapy. She wanted her children. She wanted her husband. She wanted the years back. She wanted her life back. The inner pain she was feeling at that moment was worse than the outer pain she endured from Blackie Boone. At one point, Mercedes didn't know how to let go. It was as if she had lost a part of her mind, a cutting away from her soul had taken place. And when their meeting was over, Mercedes was put in a strait jacket, dragged away screaming and crying. Her life was inconsistent. There were factors that did not add up, no means for existing --- and at that moment, her purpose was aborted.

Chapter 11

_____

Change Your Face

For about six weeks, Mercedes had been in a terrible state of stress while trying to cope with her reality. Things had changed around her and she did not know it yet. She had spent a lot of time alone and isolated from everyone else while trying to recover --- and recover she did.

By the time Mercedes had come back into her sane place, the women of the Dupree Plantation had been transferred to her facility, and for the past six weeks, Mercedes was oblivious to the changes that had taken place. She was still not her normal self, but was a lot better. She was capable of functioning with everyday duties, but not well enough to start her groups sessions again. At one point, she went through one on one counseling. She had to learn to deal with her present reality and learn how to accept that the past would never be her reality again. She was learning how to create a new future, to begin again and make that work for herself. She had to rediscover her purpose in order to help others find their own. All of this was helping her to heal and regain her inner strength.

On a day when she was allowed to have full access of the facility, she saw how things had really changed in her absence. Mercedes noticed that the facility had gotten a new image of beautification. There were blooming flowers on every corner and new trees had been planted as well. The sidewalks had been upgraded and that made the walking surface easier to walk on. All that she saw made her want to see more.

As she walked behind the facility where the pond was, she saw that benches and more trees had been put there, making it a more relaxed place. Mercedes decided to go and take advantage of the new changes as she assumed no one would be there but her. She really wanted that alone time in such a serene calm place.

But as she walked closer to where she would sit, she looked off to her left and saw a woman sitting in the distance. The sight of the woman seemed familiar to her, but Mercedes was not sure at first. As she got a little closer, she could see the silver haired woman sitting on the bench doing a familiar thing. Her mouth was moving and her eyes were closed. She was praying. Mercedes didn't want to disturb the woman, but she couldn't help it. The closer she got to the woman, the clearer it was to who this woman was. It was Sweet Helena.

Excitement welled up inside of Mercedes, but before she could move a step further or say one word, Sweet Helena said, "I've been waiting awhile for you." There was nothing else left for Mercedes to do but go and embrace her longtime friend. She had missed her, and was over joyed to see her there. Sweet Helena was the last piece to Mercedes' healing.

Mercedes kept a tight grip on Sweet Helena's hand and asked, "How long have you been here?"

"I been here for a month now. Been waiting on you to come back from wherever you decided to go. I just been sitting here, watching this place change --- hoping that some changing was going on in you too. But I see prayer sho' did help."

Mercedes listened quietly to Sweet Helena, attentive to every word that came out of her wrinkled mouth. She spoke out of the wisdom of her years and experiences, which made Mercedes see things in a different way. Mercedes then realized that she was not the only one who had lost something of great value that she loved. Her husband and children were stitched to her soul, but then a great ripping tore them apart. However, she had managed to take so much pain and abuse when she was on the Dupree Plantation, but seeing her husband for the first time in so many years, gave her a false hope of returning to the same life she had been taken from.

Sweet Helena's talks was life to Mercedes. She took her down a path in her life that she had never been. Sweet Helena told her stories of her past and how she had to raise her daughter Shuggie on a prison plantation. She told her how she didn't have a chance or choice. Even though she was born there, she was sold to the plantation just so the rest of her family could eat and have a place to stay.

"It didn't kill me on the outside", said Sweet Helena, "but killed the weak things in me, the things that would let me die. When I survived one of the harshest winters the north could send, that's when I realized God had made women to be strong. When many of the men took sick, it was us women who had to nurse them back to health, and yet many of them abuse us for their selfish lusts --- no thank you's or appreciation. The only appreciation we get is what the horses and cows get. That's why you gotta use that that's in you. My Shuggie didn't have that. She fed on the weakness and let ole Blackie Boone kill her. He didn't just kill her once, but he killed her every day until she was no more."

Sweet Helena then turned and looked Mercedes in the eyes and said, "Now that you have overcome the outside and the inside, it's time for you to put a new face on. Take that one off."

Even though Sweet Helena was talking metaphorically, Mercedes knew exactly what she was saying. There were still women coming come in and out of prison and would need someone to pour some kind of hope in them. But the only way she was going to be able to do that would be by getting herself back into becoming, becoming who she was meant to be from the beginning and making sure she got back to why she had been moved to the new Louisiana facility in the first place. She had to remind herself that she had moved the heart of the governor and made it possible for a whole system to be broken for the women to see that there was hope for a better future.

Knowing that she had her friend and mentor by her side, Mercedes wasted no time getting herself ready for the work ahead of her. When it was time for her to go to her counseling session, she made sure that was her last session. Before she went, Mercedes took her time to take down her corn-rows and pick her hair out. When she was finished, she had a big beautiful Afro. She looked at herself in the mirror and adored her new look. And at that moment, she was satisfied with what she was seeing.

When she was to begin her group sessions again, there were questions about her sanity. The facility was concerned about releasing her back as the leader of the group sessions, not wanting to lose the funding for the program. Mercedes was informed that if they lost the funding, no other programs would be coming to their facility. Therefore, in order to keep the funding and the program, she had to prove herself competent --- and prove herself, she did. This opportunity afforded Mercedes to go far and beyond her imagination. Not only did she prove herself in one capacity, she showed the facility and the great state of Louisiana her unlimited potential.

By the end of three months, Mercedes had inspired almost all the women at the facility. Sweet Helena was proud of her and encouraged Mercedes in every way. Not only did she encourage her, she kept her from getting too proud and pomp. Every now and then, Sweet Helena reminded her that she was still in a prison. Sometimes she would ask her what her plans were for when she got out. For a long time, Mercedes' answers would be, "I don't know." But Sweet Helena would tell Mercedes that there is life outside of prison and things had changed since they had been incarcerated. Honestly, Mercedes didn't have a vision for the rest of her life. She hadn't thought that far. She was only concerned with the tasks at hand.

This led Mercedes on a search for answers. She would ask the new women questions about the outside, things like "What's the latest music?" or "how much does a loaf of bread cost?' The questions were small because these were small town girls and not many of them had been out of their counties or parishes. But Mercedes had no idea how far her talents would take her, nor how far she would launch women to reach their full potential.

Getting to know the outside world while listening and encouraging the women was Mercedes' goal for the rest of her time in prison. She had brought about such a great change with the program that the Governor expanded the program allowing room for the women to incorporate business skills into their daily living. There were classes of all types, such as sewing, cooking, gardening, mechanics, beauty and hair, painting, and ceramic/pottery. For the rest of Mercedes' years in prison, she managed to take all the classes successfully. She was so free inside the prison that she took every opportunity she saw, which helped her gain many skills for a successful life after prison.

Chapter 12
─────────
The Release

The countdown had begun for Mercedes' release. The prison had given the women choices to where they wanted to be released when their time was up. Some of the women had their families to go to, but some had nowhere to go. There were a few boarding housing available around the state and the neighboring state of Mississippi.

It was a long time coming for the women. Most of them had endured the harsh conditions of the Dupree Plantation and the conditions at the new state facility felt like heaven. There was no fear of being carried off into the night or fear of raped and abused. The only thing the facility had to worry about were a few squabbles amongst the women --- nothing to serious.

Excitement and fear waged war inside of Mercedes while she waited for her six month countdown to her release. Her dear friend Sweet Helena had been gone for about three months and Mercedes impatiently waited to hear from her. She told her she would write and let her know which boarding house she had went to, but within those months, Mercedes had not heard a word. Anxiety had set in. It was not because she didn't want to go from the prison, it was because she had nothing to go back to. Her family was no more and she had to learn how to live a normal life again.

It had seemed that Mercedes had come to her last milestone in life because she couldn't see anything else ahead. She could only see prison life. She had learned to adapt to any situation, whether it was harsh or fair. No matter where life had taken her, she made her spaces a home.

The six month release date for Mercedes was like a long waiting period. It reminded her of her first day at the Dupree Plantation --- how she felt alone and betrayed. And now, the feelings of being lost and taken out of her familiar place was making themselves known to her again. The only thing that would give her a little peace and soulful rest would be a word from her dear friend Sweet Helena --- and she did hear from her eventually.

It was two months later that a letter finally came from Sweet Helena. The post marked date had been marked January 22, 1969, two months after Sweet Helena's release. Mercedes was happy to hear from her and to know that all was well with her, but couldn't understand why the letter had taken so long to reach her.

Upon opening the letter, Mercedes could smell the familiarity of her friend. Calmness begin to fill her soul once more as she read the letter. It was filled with instructions about how to begin a life outside of prison. As usual, Sweet Helena poured her wisdom into Mercedes, as the words jumped off the pages and empowered her soul once again. She didn't leave Mercedes without a destination. She told her that most of the women had scattered to different places including boarding houses in Mississippi, and that's where she was, in South Haven, Mississippi.

When Mercedes finally got news of where Sweet Helena was, she immediately went and put in for the South Haven boarding house. Sweet Helena had helped her make her mind up on where she would be moving to next. There were no questions to ask nor any changing of the mind. Mercedes had always felt as if Sweet Helena was her guardian angel, sent to help guide her along the way. So far, she had not led her wrong and she knew South Haven was where she needed to be.

As the months gradually came to an end, there were bittersweet moments. She had made a whole new family with the women in the facility. She wanted to stay, then again, she knew she had to go. Mercedes knew she would be able to do more good outside of prison as well as she did on the inside.

There was so much love poured out on Mercedes. Almost every day, there was something waiting in her room for her --- from new clothes that the women made themselves, to fresh pastries and artwork. There was no end to the love and appreciation the women and the facility had shown her. Mercedes had touched so many lives and their lives touched hers as well.

Before she left the Louisiana State Prison, most of the women asked her which boarding house she would be going to. When Mercedes told them where, most of the women went immediately and filled their papers out for the same place. So she knew she might be able to see some of them again.

Soon the last day of her twenty year sentence had come. The night before, Mercedes hardly slept a wink. She was too excited and anxious. Before she could get up, there were a slew of women standing at her door waiting to see her off. Some were in tears and smiles, and others wore a sad face. Either way, Mercedes saw the love and appreciation from each of them. She had packed most of her things, however, the things she had not packed didn't take long to get together. The women helped Mercedes load her things in the van, and finally, she was on her way.

As she looked out the window, she could see the waving women, the kisses blown, and the beautiful people she was leaving behind. As the van got farther and farther away, Mercedes went and sat on the back seat to see the women until she could see them no more.

For about a two hour drive, she sat on that same seat, teary eyed. It wasn't that she was sad, nor happy. Mercedes didn't know how she was feeling really. The time and the ride gave her a lot of time to think. She wanted to see her children, she wanted to see Sweet Helena, she wanted to be with her husband, and most of all she wanted her life back. So much was going through her mind. She wanted to know who was the woman her husband married and had put over her children. She wanted to know what ever happened to her little white baby and their family as well. Mercedes knew time had gone by and her children and her white baby were all grown up. She probably wouldn't recognize them at that point.

There were a few stops made along the way from Louisiana to Mississippi. The gas stops were well needed for bathroom breaks. Mercedes didn't need any food or snacks because the women at the facility had packed her all kinds of homemade goodies. But one thing troubled her heart as she interacted with the people, and that was the fact that racism was still alive and well. She encountered the looks and the slurs, not understanding the events that had taken place in the areas they were going through and the events in the nation.

There were the Freedom Riders murders, Martin Luther King's assassination, Medgar Evers' assassination, the Black Panther Party, the President's assassination, the riots, the hangings, the silent messages in poetry writings and the loud messages in the music. There were many things Mercedes would have to become familiar with. She would find out that the outside of prison had become worse than the inside. But the times were also changing. Nothing would stay the same. The era was just showing that things get worse before they get better, and so was it going to be with Mercedes as well.

Later, Mercedes could hear the tires on the van screech as they came to an abrupt stop.

She was still sitting in the back of the van and could not see why or what had caused them to stop. Then she could hear loud chanting in the distance, and when she stood up, she could see that they were in a line filled with angry impatient motorists who were ready to speed up and be on their way. But the wait wasn't too long. Soon, the van began to move slowly and Mercedes moved over closer to the windows to see what had happened. She got an eye full as they went across the Mississippi boarder only to see men dressed in white sheets, demonstrating their love for their organization.

As Mercedes looked on at the demonstrators, it was as if someone took a hammer and hit her in the stomach. All her memories of the night she was dragged out of her bed flooded her soul once more. She became nervous and tried to hold it together as they continued to ride towards their destination. The scene was rehearsed over and over in her mind as her hands began to tremble. But she knew that once she had reached South Haven, she would be okay because Sweet Helena would make it all better. She knew that Sweet Helena would have some words of comfort and some wonderful words of wisdom for her.

And so, after hours of riding, Mercedes was arriving in the city of South Haven, Mississippi. It was a small place, but with all the construction that was going on, she could tell it was a growing place. The boarding house was not far from town. It was in walking distance and so thought of as a good thing for morning walks.

As the van pulled in the driveway, Mercedes was eager to see her friend Sweet Helena, and at the same time nervous about starting a new life in a new place. As she began to unload the van, she repeatedly looked towards the door of the boarding house, hoping to see Sweet Helena standing there. Instead, she saw other women gathering on the porch and crowding her way, and even though she had not seen Sweet Helena yet, she did see some familiar faces including Eula. While passing through the crowded force of women, Mercedes knew how to feel towards the friendly faces of welcoming smiles, but really didn't know how to feel towards the bland stares.

Eula grabbed some of Mercedes' bags and shouted to the other women, "Y'all stop staring at her and help with these bags! Y'all know how we do it round here."

Eula's enthusiastic personality made Mercedes giggle a bit under her breath, but she smiled and looked on as the women began getting in a hurry to grab something --- anything.

"They standing around here like they ain't never seen a new woman come to this boarding house", Eula continued. "I been here for about three months and the women been in and out of here so quick." Then she turned and look at Mercedes with a big smile and said, "Ceddi (Sadie), you gone love it here."

Mercedes heard her, but then again, she didn't because she was looking for her friend.

"Where Sweet Helena? She said she would meet me here." Mercedes looked up at Eula and saw that her countenance had changed. "What's wrong with you?" Mercedes stopped what she was doing and waited on Eula to answer her.

"You don't know, do you?" Eula stopped what she was doing and took Mercedes by the hand and continued, "Sweet Helena passed away in her sleep about three months ago. The doctors said it was natural causes."

Mercedes' eyes began to fill with tears. At that moment, there was no end to her pain. She felt lost, confused, and angry all over again. She didn't know how to react. Out of the emotional distress, she wondered how Sweet Helena could leave her like that. They had plans --- plans to make a better future, to show Mercedes how to navigate through life outside of prison.

Mercedes sat down with tears in her eyes again and pain all over her. Eula did her best to console her, but somehow Mercedes seemed to gain un-measurable strength as she sat there thinking --- thinking about how Sweet Helena was not a loss in her life. She had helped her gain so much by teaching her wonderful things and imparting wonderful wisdom in her life.

Mercedes looked at Eula and said, "Well, I guess this is a new chapter and another road I'll have to learn how walk down. Sweet Helena is with me even as I speak. She'll never leave me. I just need some time alone. Let me grieve."

For a few minutes, it looked as if Eula was not going to leave, but she eventually left Mercedes to think about Sweet Helena and the journey they had together. She thought about Sweet Helena's daughter, Shuggie, and how she had a beautiful heart also. The memories led her to think about the women she had loved and lost at the hands of Blackie Boone. She thought about how Sweet Helena would tell her it's time to move on from the past and gain a new future, and a new future she would.

Mercedes had accomplished so much in prison by helping the women find purpose and meaning in their lives, and she would continue to do the same. She didn't know the challenge ahead, but she was willing to face any adversity at that point.

By the time Mercedes had finished her phase of grief, hours had passed and the sun was setting. There was a smell in the air and it smelled familiar. The women had cooked supper for the evening and was preparing for her to come join in. When Mercedes joined them, all eyes were on her. She wasn't nervous or timid because she knew all too well the company of many women. What she didn't know was, how Eula had painted a wonderful, glorious picture of who she was. So, some of the women were waiting to see their heroine of grace.

As Mercedes sat at the plentiful table, she stared at all the food before her. She questioned on the inside of her and wondered did they eat like this every day. But before she could finish her thoughts, Eula spoke up and said, "We usually don't eat like this, but because you have made it here, we wanted to make this a special evening for you. It's what Sweet Helena would've wanted."

Mercedes smiled as she held back her tears. She stood up and gave a silent "Thank you" accompanied by a bow. Eula went over and gave Mercedes a big hug and soon all the other women followed. There was nothing but love in the house that night. Mercedes felt so welcomed while also feeling Sweet Helena's presence. She didn't feel alone, but nothing could replace the reality of wanting to be home with her children and husband. Those are the ones she really wanted to see when she got out of prison. But a substitute family was what she had to appreciate at that moment.

Chapter 13

The Debut

As Mercedes settled in, she began to tour the large boarding house. She took her time and studied each woman, carefully examining their habits and ways. There were both black and white women, each with a story to tell and each with relatable problems. No one treated the other any different from the other. She saw how Eula had grown and had taken her gift to make money. She allowed her talent to make room for her as women from town would come and get their hair dressed by her.

Mercedes saw how Eula was making a living, but she wondered what the other women were doing to get by. She would soon find out that some of the women had started selling themselves to men. That didn't set well with Mercedes. After all, that's how many of the women ended up in prison in the first place. Mercedes began to think hard every day on how she would try and bring change to the women's lives. She had to get them to see themselves differently and the only way to do that, was to get them to think differently. She knew it would take time because she had just gotten there and didn't want the women to think she was bringing an iron fist to rule them.

The boarding house was sitting on five acres of beautiful land with a large field perfect for flowers. It was clear, with pine trees lining the property but there was one other house next to the boarding house. It was not on the property, but just over the property line. The house looked run down a bit, but not an eye sore. Each morning, Mercedes would sit on the front porch, drink her coffee and look over at the house, and each week a delivery man would come and bring a box of groceries to the house. Mercedes never saw who lived there, but she would hear a man's voice yell, "Come on in."

And as the weeks went on, the boxes began to pile up on the porch. One box turned into three boxes, and three boxes turned into five boxes, until finally, Mercedes asked Eula, "Who lives in that house over there?"

Eula said she didn't know. "I've heard rumors that it's an old man who had lost his job and got sick. He can't do for himself, but no one will hardly go over there 'cause he's so mean and hateful."

"Is he black or white?" Mercedes wanted to know because if he was black, it would be easier on the rumors if she decided to go over to try and check on the man. If he was white, she didn't want anything to do with him, only because she didn't want to end up back in jail.

"Honey, times are changing", Eula said confidently. "Colored folks are changing the way the world see them."

Mercedes smiled and replied, "Yea, but this colored gal ain't taking no chances." And they both laughed with no discourtesy towards each other.

There were times when Mercedes sat thinking over and over about the old man in the house and wondered how she was going to go over there to make sure he was okay. She didn't want the man to be dead in the house and no one knew he was decaying. She was brave, but she was also fearful. Everything was new and different outside of prison. She was free, but wanted to use her freedom wisely. She had heard the times were changing, but her past experiences with society had not changed her mind much.

Before the beginning of a new week, Mercedes rose early in the morning and prepared herself to go over and check on the old man. She took a headband and pulled her Afro back, went and got Eula for support. Quietly, they walked the gravel driveway together. As they walked on the porch, they met a few raccoon who had made it their business to help themselves to the food in the boxes left on the porch.

Mercedes knocked on the door and called out, "Hello! Just came by to check on you sir." no one answered. Mercedes called out again and again. Then, she heard some kind of movement. Eula had gone to a window and saw the old man lying on the floor. That was the only indicator Mercedes needed in order to go in and try to help.

Upon entering the house, the women were gagged with the stench of the closed house and body wasted. There were boxes of groceries with rotting food as well as canned foods. They moved closer to the old man and could see his black feet sticking out from behind his leather recliner.

Mercedes called out again, "Sir, are you alright?" The man grunted while moving his feet a little. The closer they got to him, they could see he had been there for a few days. He had lain in his waste for some time and the stench helped the women cover their mouths and noses as they contained themselves from vomiting.

At first, Eula was at the head of the man and Mercedes was at the feet. Mercedes could not see the face until she moved in a little closer. Her eyes bucked at the sight of who he was. It was ole Blackie Boone laying there like an old dying dog. A stroke had taken him down, knocking him off the throne of his pride. Mercedes ran out of the house and back on the porch, taking deep breathes as memories flashed before her. Eula followed behind and asked what the matter was.

Taking deeper breathes, Mercedes answered, "That's the demon from hell who was sent to torment me for so many years on the Dupree Sugar Plantation."

"Well, what are we gone do with that demon now?" Eula was concerned, but was willing to do whatever Mercedes wanted.

Mercedes closed the door and said, "I don't know just yet. Do he look like he can make it another day in there?" Eula replied, "Yes, I think so."

Mercedes walked off the porch and said, "Good. I'll think of something by tomorrow. I need time to think about this."

That night, Mercedes took the time to look at herself in the mirror. It had been years since she had just looked at herself all over. The sight of Blackie Boone brought back the horrors and pains of the past. She undressed herself slowly as her eyes gazed on all the old scars he had left on her body. She knew they would never go away. They were there as reminders of the Dupree Plantation and all it stood for. The scars led from her stomach to legs. She opened her legs only to see more scars. She turned around and saw scars on her back and buttocks --- little scars and big scars, she could remember how and when she got each one.

When Mercedes had lain down for bed, she hoped sleep would evade her, but it didn't. She dreamed of her dear friend Sweet Helena. She was in the house where she and Eula had found ole Blackie Boone. Sweet Helena was more beautiful than ever, looking like a picture of youth. The house was beautiful as well with all kinds of women coming in and out the door. Sweet Helena was trying to tell her something in the dream. She asked Mercedes, "What are you willing to sacrifice?" After that, Mercedes was awakened to the bright morning sun. It took her a minute to gather her thoughts as to figure out was it real or a dream. A quiet knock followed, only to be Eula inquiring about what to do about ole Blackie Boone. The dream was a sign on what Mercedes should do. So the two headed back over there.

This time they didn't knock, but they cautiously walked in and made their way to ole Blackie Boone. Making sure he was still alive, Mercedes gave instructions while she and Eula took their time to get him in the recliner chair. It was not easy lifting up over 300 pounds of dead weight. When they had gotten him settled in the chair, the women quickly made their way to the front porch for fresh air. The fresh stench of urine and feces almost suffocated them. When Mercedes had contained herself, she told Eula they were gonna need some help, but not just any help. She needed women she could trust. She didn't need women with sticky fingers or women with an unjust agenda, and if they found anything important, they were to report it to her. Eula knew exactly what Mercedes meant and knew two of the women who were perfect candidates, Willie Jean and Ms. Merlee.

Mercedes trusted Eula's choices of women and asked no questions as she continued to give instruction. They were to begin their work at night, cleaning up ole Blackie Boone and his house. Looking at the filth, Mercedes knew they had plenty of work to do. She didn't quite know what to do about getting help for Blackie Boone's health at that point. She and Eula took their time to find him some clean clothes and get him cleaned up, but the utility bills had not been paid so there was no way for the water-pump to carry water inside the house.

But that was no big task for the women. Willie Jean and Merlee got buckets and carried water inside and filled the tub for Blackie Boone, while Eula and Mercedes searched and prodded, cleaned and swept, for nothing was left private for Blackie Boone.

When they had gotten him in the tub, Mercedes asked to be left alone with Blackie Boone. She dipped her hand in the tub and watched Blackie Boone as he shivered to the coldness of the water. Mercedes sat there for a minute looking at him and he stared back with his crooked face.

"Yea, you know exactly who I am. Bet you never thought of seeing me again. To be honest, I never ever wanted to see you again."

Mercedes grabbed soap and towel and began to talk some more. She moved in a little closer and said, "Ain't it funny how this thing called life can change on ya? You wanna know some truth? I know I been through some changes that helped me know what hate really was. God knows I hated you. I hated we ever crossed paths. Now that's some truth for ya. I know a lot, how you sent a death certificate to my family declaring me dead. But here I am."

Blackie Boone said nothing to Mercedes, not because he didn't want to, but because he couldn't. The severity of the stroke left him speechless and demobilized. He just stared at Mercedes while she talked and washed his body, but when she looked up at him, she saw a tear began to run down his face. Nothing prepared her for that. She stopped what she was doing and asked Eula if she and the others could finish washing him.

She went outside and sat under the night sky and looked up at the stars. She began to pray within herself, hoping that her secret prayer would reach heaven that very night. When she had returned, the women had cleaned Blackie Boone up and was ready to dress him for bed. All the while, he kept his eyes on Mercedes as he watched her closely. She would see him, but didn't let it distract her. The women carefully dressed him for bed and made him comfortable as possible. Mercedes assured him that they would be back the next day to check on him. Blackie Boone blinked his eyes and Mercedes closed the door.

Each day, the women would get together and go do some type of work at Blackie Boone's house. In the mornings, they would get him out of bed, make sure he was clean, and get him fed. In the evenings, they would pretty much do the same thing. He was not stubborn towards the women, it seemed that he was happy they were there and welcomed their company. They even took the time to move him around, opening and closing his hands, lifting his arms, and helping him to stand and sit. At first, it was challenging for him. He would break out in big balls of sweat while attempting to help the women out with his limited exercises. It was alright with them because they knew it was the only way he would get better and stronger.

There were good days and bad days for Blackie Boone. Some days the ladies would get there and he would have fecal matter all over the place and some days he would not. Some days he would cooperate and some days he would be as stubborn as a mule. Sometimes, Willie Jean and Merlee would wrestle with him, until he would see Mercedes pass by or come in the room. Their care started to make him stronger over the course of time and he was displaying it every day.

One evening, Mercedes made her way over to his house. She had gone to the general store and bought a few things for him. When she made it there, he was sitting in his old recliner staring out the window. Mercedes walked in front of him and said, "I got you a few things from the general store. I hope you like 'em."

She started pulling the things out one by one --- a pair of britches, a long sleeve white shirt, a walking cane, some pencils for writing, and a handful of mints that Mercedes told him he was not gonna eat all at once. Blackie Boone looked at each of the things and gave her a half of a smile while Mercedes seemed to entertain him with what she had bought.

Time had started healing old wombs for her and him. Mercedes didn't see him as the menacing, hell raising man as before. She had no fear of him anymore either. She only saw him as a lost, helpless soul and finally realized what her dream of Sweet Helena really meant. "What are you willing to sacrifice?" Those were the words of her dear friend speaking to her from a place not found on earth. She was still guiding her with her wisdom as if she had never left her.

Mercedes talked with Blackie Boone until the sun went down. It was almost time for Eula, Merlee, and Willie to come over and help put him to bed. As Mercedes attempted to leave,

Blackie Boone caught her by the arm. He had a firm grip while looking her in the eyes.

Mercedes looked at him intently and asked, "What is it? Are you trying to say something?" Blackie Boone blinked his eyes faster than he had ever blinked, letting Mercedes know the matter was important. He took his good arm and pointed to the wall by the chimney. Mercedes looked puzzled, then she got up and went to where he was pointing. At first, she didn't notice anything out of the ordinary. She looked back at Blackie Boone and he was still pointing, so she looked again, carefully. She saw a crack, just big enough to slide her small lady-like fingers through. After then, she knew what to do. She gave a hard pull and the wall opened into a small closet. Not only did the closet open, but Mercedes' eyes opened wider than ever before at the sight of what she was seeing. Wall to wall was money and legal papers. In disbelief, Mercedes walked in slowly. She had never seen so much money in her life, especially not a colored person.

She looked at Blackie Boone and asked, "Where did you get all this money from?" He looked at her and pointed to the pencils she had just bought. Mercedes hurried and got a pencil and a piece of paper. Her curiosity was burning to know the answer. She fixed the pencil in his hand and held the paper steady as he wrote, "I want you to have it." Mercedes was shocked at what she was seeing. Her heart was beating faster and faster in unbelief as he kept writing. "Find legal papers. I'll sign them."

"What are you saying? Are you sure?" Mercedes was so in awe and kind of confused about all the things that was taking place at that moment. She didn't know if she should jump for joy, tell someone, or just keep it to herself. Blackie Boone kept writing and finally said, "You took care of me --- how I treated you." Mercedes grabbed him by the hand and just held it. His tears fell softly, and so did hers. Pride had been sacrificed and love had won a victory of a lifetime.

Upon hearing the others approaching. Mercedes quickly closed the small closet. She and Blackie Boone would find the time to take care of all matters. But at that moment, it was to be kept as is. Mercedes had to ponder the events of that evening. There was much to consider and much to be done. She was not dead, and her secret prayers were answered.

Chapter 14

Our Ordinary Eyes

By the end of the Nixon presidency, Mercedes had moved into her own. Blackie Boone had transferred all power and rights of his property and lands to her, making her one of the only colored women in the county with an abundance of land and wealth. In such a short time, she had acquired a lot. She put it to great use, and as usual she thought of others more than herself. She turned Blackie Boone's old home into her own boarding house for women. It was not just for the women who came out of prison, it was for all women who had been through a traumatic crisis. She had started her group sessions and became a partner with the Louisiana facility and the Mississippi prison system for women.

The Vietnam War was coming to an end and it was sending home a lot of broken men. Eventually, the broken men were coming home and breaking their women. Some women stayed with their broken men, trying to work beyond the pain, but some women left and found their way to Mercedes. So many women found peace and solace when they saw the sign "Mercedes' Boarding House for Women", and every spring, the fields along the road leading up to the boarding house would be full of beautiful flowers setting the tone for the big house with the beautiful wrap-around porch. And even though it was a boarding house for women, Blackie Boone was the only man living there amongst the women.

Over the years, many women had come and gone, but no one knew their real story but he and Mercedes. Eula had gone on to make her own life. She put her hair dressing skills to use and became successful in Memphis, TN. Not only did Eula become successful, but many women took their time to go through a healing process by attending Mercedes' group sessions. Sometimes Mercedes would look around at all the women moving throughout the house and would think to herself how beautiful they all were. There they were, black and white, and no one judged the other according to their race. They all saw each other as they saw themselves, taking the time to help where needed. Mercedes never thought she would have found herself at a place of comfort while all kinds of gracious gifts would come for her in the mail. Women who had benefited from her kindness sent all kinds of things back to her --- gifts of thanksgiving. Those were her flowers, beautiful and unique just like each woman.

Mercedes had met many women. She helped to change their lives and in the process, they helped shape hers as well. The boarding house was a big one. It had five bedrooms, but she only used four to help board the women. The other room was for Mercedes alone, so by the time someone had sent her a reference for another woman, the house was full. It could only house twelve women at a time and she was not intending on having anyone in her room.

Mercedes didn't just have women from the prisons, but she also had women from abusive relationships. Sometimes she would get only one letter from a woman seeking shelter, and sometimes she would get more than one from one woman.

One morning, everyone was still asleep except Mercedes. She had been awake already waiting on the sunrise before her feet hit the floor. She had lain there thinking and would whisper a small prayer every now and then. She could hear the sounds of life beginning to stir for the day and the old and young men's trucks crank for their early start of work. Then, she heard it. It was a light tap on the front door. No one heard it but Mercedes. It was a knock that would change her life and open up old memories.

She walked quietly to the front door, but first peeped out the window to get a glance of who would be knocking on her door so early in the morning. When she opened the door, it was a young white woman who looked like she had been thrown out of a car and run over. She had bruises on one side of her face and her arm was in a sling. There was no way Mercedes could turn her away. She knew this woman would need some type of care and some type of soul healing.

Mercedes invited her in, sat her down at the kitchen table, and made her a nice warm cup of coffee. She also fixed herself a cup and sat down in front of the woman.

"What's your name child?" Mercedes asked very cautiously because she could relate to how the woman was feeling.

"My name is Kathy McClain", the woman answered. At first, the name nor the face was familiar to Mercedes, but it would soon become apparent to who was sitting in front of her. She did not recognize the woman's face because of the bruises, but her eyes did look familiar.

Mercedes went on to ask, "What happened to ya?"

Kathy went on to answer, "Well, I had been married for six years. The first year was a good one, but soon turned into misery with drinking and the women."

"Any children from the union", asked Mercedes.

Kathy sadly looked up at Mercedes and answered, "None living. He beat three of 'em out of me."

As they sat at the table, Mercedes wondered what to do with the poor soul. She knew there wasn't any room in the other rooms, and she knew she couldn't turn her away, so she decided to the only thing she knew, and that was put Kathy in the room with her. She didn't want to keep asking her questions without caring for her at the same time. Mercedes took her to the room and gave her something clean to put on and prepared a bath for her. When Kathy took her clothes off, Mercedes saw how someone had done a number on her. She had bruises on her stomach and back. She had been wrapped up because of broken ribs. It was painful for Kathy to raise her arms, so Mercedes decided to cut the undershirt off of her.

For about two weeks, Mercedes and the women took care of Kathy. Kathy loved the atmosphere and how the women were learning skills for business. She also saw how they loved Mercedes and how grateful they were for her. The women made money by selling their arts and crafts, and they went across the border at times to Memphis and sold their honey, clothes, quilts, and crops to local markets. It was a little easier for them to sell across the border than in Mississippi.

When the women had gone and the house was quiet, Mercedes brought Blackie Boone on the front porch for morning air and sat down to enjoy it herself. Kathy joined them as she took a deep breath of the clean air that blew across her face. "There is nothing like a good country breeze", Kathy said with a smile.

"No it's not", responded Mercedes.

"You ever wonder where it goes when it leaves us?"

Mercedes leaned back in her chair and thought about it for a minute and said, "I don't really know. Maybe it comes right back to us. It may take a week or a year, but it probably finds it way right back here."

Then, there were no more words for a while as the three of them enjoyed the morning and watched the cars drive by. But after a while, Kathy broke the silence and asked, "Why yo' mama named you Mercedes?"

Mercedes giggled at the thought and the question, and answered, "Because I was born in the back seat of a Mercedes Benz. It wasn't my mother's doing, it was my father who did the naming."

Kathy said nothing to Mercedes' response. Instead, she said, "I know who you are."

Mercedes looked over at Kathy and said, "Oh, you do huh? How's that?"

"You were my Nana", Kathy replied softly.

Blackie Boone turned his head towards both of the women and waited on a response from Mercedes, but she was speechless at first.

"I'm Kathryn Grace. As I grew older, people started calling me Kathy, especially in high school. Then I married and got the last name McClain."

Mercedes was stunned at the news and asked, "How long you been knowing who I was?"

"I knew who you were before I was referenced to this place. I had followed you while you were in the Louisiana State Facility. I had heard of how you were helping the women find themselves, and after all you had been through."

Kathy went on to tell Mercedes her story as she and Blackie Boone sat in silence to listen. There was excitement and then there was pain of absence. The absence of Mercedes' husband and children, absence of thoughts of another woman raising her children as Kathy told her how she grew up with them and how they turned out to be great adults. Mercedes found out that they had married and she was a grandmother. Kathryn Grace was the beginning of her problems, but now she hoped that she would help bring closure to all the time she had missed with her past.

When Mercedes started talking, she had so many questions. She wanted to know if Kathy could get in touch with them, and sure enough, she could. Kathy had found phone numbers and addresses for Mercedes and the process had begun. At first, Mercedes wanted to call each one of her children, but fear stopped her words. So she decided to sit down and write each of them a letter, and at the end of each letter, she put her phone number. By the time she decided to put the letters in the mail, she hoped for good responses from all of them. It was only time that stood between the outcomes. And time seemed to torture Mercedes.

Every time the phone rung, her heart would beat fast and excitement would overrule her at the thought of maybe one of her children would call. The mail would be thoroughly examined in hopes that one would write.

But after a month, the phone did ring and it was for her. Mercedes was not in the house, instead she was in the "Field of Beautiful Flowers". She had planted the flowers shortly after Blackie Boone had signed the property over to her, and every year, beautiful colorful flowers would bloom from spring to summer and early fall.

As she walked through the field, Mercedes could hear a voice in the distance calling her name. When she turned around, she could see Kathy running and shouting. When she had finally arrived to Mercedes, Kathy was out of breath. "Catch your breath child and then talk to me", Mercedes instructed.

Kathy huffed and puffed a few times and finally got the words out. "It's the phone. Collect call from Baton Rouge. I think it's one of your children."

Mercedes didn't ask any questions. She took off running to the house. Even though she was in her late forties, her legs were good to her at that moment. She ran so fast that she left Kathy behind, who refused to run but walk instead. When Mercedes made it to the house, all the women were standing around waiting with one of them holding the phone ready to hand it to her. Everyone was excited and curious because they knew this was something that Mercedes wanted more than anything in the world.

Mercedes slowly put the phone to her ear, not saying anything at first. She listened to the breathing on the other end and the sound of children and adult voices in the background. Finally, with a shiver in her voice, she said, "Hello".

Not only was it one of her children, but it was all of her children and grandchildren. All the women, including Kathy, watched as

Mercedes laughed and cried while she talked on the phone. There seemed to be no resentment from them, but joy and happiness knowing that she was alive and well.

God had answered her prayers. It had seemed like a lifetime, but God had answered her prayers. The boarding house was filled with laughter and rejoicing, until there was a knock at the door. Kathy told the women that she would answer it while Mercedes continued to catch up with her children. Just as Mercedes was hanging up the phone, Kathy opened the door and met a bullet to the face. The sound of a gunshot had paralyzed everyone in the house. It was Kathy's husband. He had tracked her down and found her. By the time Kathy's body hit the floor, Mercedes had grabbed a pistol from off the wall and shot him for every bruise, scar, and broken bone he had rendered to Kathy's body. She didn't think twice about the outcome. She only saw ONE of her.

It was Blackie Boone who started to write as one of the women took the gun out of Mercedes hand and sat her down. When Blackie Boone had finished writing, he handed the paper to Mercedes and Mercedes handed it to one of the women. It was instructions, and none of the women had a problem following them. Some grabbed soap and water and others grabbed shovels and headed to the "Field of Beautiful Flowers". They individually wrapped each body and buried them in the field. Kathy was buried on one end of the field and her husband was buried on the other side in an unmarked grave. But Kathy was buried with lilies topping her grave so Mercedes would always know where she was. After that, no one spoke of the events. They let the sleeping dead lay.

And so, life went on. Mercedes had blood on her hands, yet she was acknowledged as a heroine of grace. She was labeled as a protector and friend. And as the years passed, the events of Kathy and her husband's deaths never traveled out of the boarding house. Mercedes was reunited with her children and their families as the holidays and birthdays were celebrated in each other's presence.

Death had also found ole Blackie Boone. He lived twenty peaceful years in the care of Mercedes and the women who had come and left the boarding house. It took a while for death to finally lay Mercedes down. She lived forty more years from her release from prison. She died in the years of her eighty's leaving a legacy behind that sparked a revolution for women's liberation. By the time of the new millennium, her story was told throughout the region and eventually the boarding house became a historical sight and landmark in the south. The "Field of Beautiful Flowers" continued to bloom each year and the flowers continued to capture the attention of all who passed through the area.

Ordinary Eyes

© 2018 Pamela Thornton

Novelist:

Brace yourself for another impactful short novel that will leave you wanting more. Pam Thornton brings an uncompromising level to her latest literary work, "Ordinary Eyes". She puts the bitter and the sweet together and gives her audience a taste of wanting more.

Releasing her 6th literary work, (one includes a study guide for teachers and students) Pam Thornton takes her readers on historical paths while providing dramatic entertainment in her literature.

Born and raised in the south, she has taken it upon herself to explore the history that made southern traditions which has given our country pride and shame. In her works, she releases the problems and solutions one may have faced throughout the making of the historical south and brings her audiences a plethora of real life fiction.

www.ingramcontent.com/pod-product-compliance
Lightning Source LLC
Chambersburg PA
CBHW070824180626
46818CB00001B/384